I0519800

Lynton
and
The Stellenbosch Terror

#13 in the Lynton Series

By

J. Wayne Frye

Notice:

The reader should remember that the seasons are
reversed in South Africa, so references to the
winter refer to July, not December.

This book is written in
Canadian English
and teachers should alert their students
to the variances in spellings.

LYNTON AND THE STELLENBOSCH TERROR

I have written many books and dedicated them to people who had a profound influence on me. This book is dedicated to a person who is my cousin, and I must admit, as a youth, I was mesmerized by her beauty and athletic ability. Today, I admire her for devotion to her son who suffered a debilitating disability. She is a woman of immense courage and unstinting determination.

TO: DAWN CAGLE TROTTER

And as always to my muse:
Lynton Globa Viñas – the dynamic dynamo.

Copyright 2017 by J. Wayne Frye
All rights reserved. No part of this book or covers may be reproduced or transmitted in any form or by any other means, electronic or mechanical, including photocopying, recording, or by any information storage and retrieval system, without permission from the author.
This is a work of fiction. Any similarity to persons living or dead is coincidental.

Catalogue Number: 971377-2017

ISBN: 978-1-928183-32-7

Fireside Books – Canadian Division
Part of the Peninsula Publishing Consortium

J. WAYNE FRYE

LYNTON AND THE STELLENBOSCH TERROR

TABLE OF CONTENTS

ABOUT THE AUTHOR

The author with the real-life Lynton Viñas

Wayne Frye's *Aaron Adams* mysteries, *Chablis Louise Chavez* thrillers, *Girl* books and *Lynton* adventures have titillated the brains of those who enjoy tantalizing tales that challenge the mind. His life, like the heroes he writes about, has been filled with adventure and excitement.

Wayne Frye has been a college hockey coach, university professor, and at one time, the youngest university president in the USA. Called a marketing genius by the *Los Angeles Times*, he has been a promotional consultant to hockey teams and motion picture companies. He has been cited for his work with inner-city gangs in Los Angeles and is active in the anti-globalization movement. A proud Canadian, he divides his time between Ladysmith, British Columbia; Laguna, Philippines and Cape Town, South Africa. He provides satirical political commentary to many Canadian newspapers.

Some of the 44 books by J. Wayne Frye

White Meteors and the Ghost of Sue Ann McGee
Hockey Mania and the Mystery of Nancy Running Elk
Something Evil in the Darkness at Hopkins House
How Hockey Saved a Jew From the Holocaust
The Girl who Rode into a Storm
The Girl Who Stirred up the Whirlwind
The Girl Who Motivated Murder Most Foul
The Girl Who Said Goodbye for the Last Time
Sammy Sasquatch and the Sts'ailes Star
Fall From Apocalypse
Armageddon Now
Worth Part 1 and Worth Part 2
When Jesus Came to Jersey as the Son of Thunder
When Jesus Came to Canada to Lead an Indigenous Rebellion
Points of Rebellion: Aboriginals Who Fought for Justice
Lynton Walks on Water
Lynton Curls Her Hair
Lynton and the Vampire at Tagaytay Manor
Lynton Buys a Cell-Phone and Hears the Voice of Doom
Lynton Viñas and Beowulf Perez in the Taal Inferno
Lynton and the Ghosts in the Mansion on Balete Drive
Lynton's South African Adventure
Lynton, the Karoo Vampire and the Jewels of Omar Bin Abi
Chablis: Avenging Angel for the Forgotten
In the City of Lost Hope
Chablis and the Terrorist
Pursuit
The Disappearance

Prologue

Face to Face with the Stellenbosch Terror

Be ye weary of any mirth!

Can you find a humble woman,

Glad to be on the green earth?

One with no greedy plan to summon,

Knowing wealth has no true worth.

Things unseen make the floor creak.

Perhaps, if you search around

You may find the one I seek;

Standing firm on shaky ground,

LYNTON AND THE STELLENBOSCH TERROR

Proud, yet modest, kind and meek.

From the evil she will not defer.
If your search discovers her,
Would you for a moment gaze?
For she is what we all prefer,
This little brown girl to amaze.

The devil is an intrepid liar.
But she is what we all should admire,
The woman the bewildered seek.
She lights hope's blazing fire.
She is Lynton Viñas, dynamic but meek.

My literary hero has always been Mickey Spillane, and my friendship with him while living in Myrtle Beach, South Carolina is embossed deep within my psyche, not because he encouraged my writing as we sat on the dock of his Merrill's Inlet home, but because he showed me how the famous and rich can, in a few cases, just be ordinary people with no tint of arrogance or self-absorption. Today's reality show media stars and successful businesspeople prance around like peacocks in full bloom, and the gullible, idol worshipping public, for some unfathomable reason, lavish attention on these banal creatures who have about as much talent and business acumen as a slug crawling across a sidewalk. In most cases, their claim-to-fame revolves around being born into privilege. The gullible public bows in homage to the creatures of wealth that are a blight on humanity and all it should represent. The oppressed simply line up for their balls and chains willingly while worshipping those who enslave them.

On the other hand, there are a few rich and famous people, like Mickey Spillane, who had a modest home and lived among the middle class. In fact, he did not even own a car. Oh, excuse me; he did have a 1942 MG that John Wayne had given him in 1952. He used it as a home for his cats. Being a New Yorker by birth, and living there most of his life, he did not even have a driver's licence. This was a man whom, at the time, ranked number two behind the Bible in all-time book sales. Yet, he saw no need for pretentiousness, and most of his friends were working class people, not the rich and famous, although there were some of those who would visit on occasion. He was a rare breed in a nation where a person's worth is far too often judged by the content of their bank account rather than the content of their character.

Alas, in a nation that spends an obscene amount on guns, bullets and weapons of mass destruction to subdue the world for exploitation by the wealthy and their corporations, while allowing its own citizens to languish in abject poverty at the highest rate in the industrialized world, it was refreshing to find one of the rich who actually had some semblance of humility. In a country that looks upon poverty as a disease, rather than the result of capitalistic exploitation, the very people who are the victims of the exploitation vote against their own self-interests because of manipulation through patriotic babble, bigotry and religious subterfuge forged by those at the top to keep the ignorant enslaved.

LYNTON AND THE STELLENBOSCH TERROR

What is my point? Simply that Lynton Viñas is the very epitome of modesty and commitment to the cause of economic and social justice in a world where it is in short supply. As a renowned and world famous demon fighter, she never exhibits self-absorption, disdain for those trapped in poverty or ever displays a lack of humbleness. Her life is devoted to standing against injustice, and she never wavers in her belief that all people, regardless of economic station, are entitled to respect. This quiet, unassuming woman never tarries in her devotion to justice.

In South Africa, she had given up on her modestly successful singing career and demon-fighting adventures to concentrate on advanced studies at the famous International Hotel School in Cape Town. Yet, her reputation as a demon hunter frequently propelled her into situations that are, as her husband says, best left for the professional authorities to solve, so that she might avoid the adventurous sojourns that cause him so much worry and consternation. However, equally known for her stubbornness and tenacity, she frequently ignores her husband's pleas for a less adventurous life.

Having just returned to Cape Town after her adventure with the ape-like wild man Barbizon, where, in the Karoo Escarpment, she had searched for buried treasure, battled blood-sucking shape-shifting vampires, fought marauding bandits and delivered a cold-bloodied killer to justice, she was ready for a rest before school started again. However, there is an old saying that there is no rest for the weary. Lynton had decided to relax by taking the steam engine pulled train from Cape Town to the countryside of Stellenbosch and enjoy the sights of this quaint town, but little did she know she was about to chug her way toward another adventure, and this time she would come face to face with the Stellenbosch terror.

Chapter 1

The Coming Terror

Spirits dance in delight,

As people tremble in the night,

Not just from outward terror,

But absent of distractions,

That propel our actions.

We are left alone

In the bleak darkness

With our thoughts.

Thus we pour the tonic

That both heals and mars,

LYNTON AND THE STELLENBOSCH TERROR

A psychological blanket,

Leaving quivering scars.

After over a year in Cape Town, Lynton had tried with all her being to lead a more sedate life, but fate was a determined hunter that kept interfering with her desire to cause her husband less worry. She had recounted to him all the sordid details of her last adventure in the Karoo Escapement with Barbizon, much to his chagrin. Still, he, as always, had a difficult time being angry with her, as, whether by *Face-Book Messenger*, *Skype* or in real face-to-face encounters, all she had to do was tilt that little head, let out that coy sigh, as her long, silky dark hair drooped over her left eye and his heart melted with love and he became putty in her hands. She knew what she was doing, but oh, she did it so well.

There are regularly scheduled trains from the Cape Town Railway Station, but Wayne had insisted she enjoy a leisurely ride on the old steam engine tourist train that plied its way to

LYNTON AND THE STELLENBOSCH TERROR

Stellenbosch, huffing and puffing its way through the magnificent countryside, allowing one to truly experience the rural beauty of South Africa in all its glory.

It was early morning and Lynton was reflecting on her past adventure in the mighty Karoo and the scintillating thrills, the overwhelming horror and the doom that seemed to be so certain at the time, as she pulled her white fur coat tightly around her fine form. Most people think anywhere in Africa is hot, humid and as you walk about there will be lions snapping at your heels, but the lower part of South Africa is almost as near frigid Antarctica as it is the humid laden equator, so they even get occasional snow there. She smiled as she thought about Simon's Town when she saw someone wearing a T-shirt with a penguin image on it. She remembered how she and Wayne went there to cavort with the penguins, and in her youthful exuberance, she had made it impossible for Wayne to keep up with her, so he fell on the rocks and cut himself on the leg, getting a serious infection.

That was the life Wayne had embraced in the arms of a much younger woman who had rekindled his own youthfulness and brought a new gloriousness to a life that had been torn asunder a few years before. She was his salvation that had lifted him from the pit of despair. Ironically, he, too, had been her salvation, as she was recovering from a bad relationship that had floundered in a tempestuous sea of raging storms. Thus, the two had forged a mutual bond of love in the sweet embrace of hope.

Lynton was usually surrounded by people, as her natural friendliness and humbleness attracted a bevy of friends who enjoyed her company, but all she wanted now was to be alone, to enjoy some tranquility free of drama as she waited for Wayne's return to her side from Canada, where he had to go, at the insistence of his publisher, on one of his hated book-signing tours. For Lynton, the past four years had been a journey of love, but because of their competing interests and careers unfortunate separations were often manifested.

LYNTON AND THE STELLENBOSCH TERROR

As she looked at the on-line news feed on her cell-phone, she thought of how the modern world had lost the real journalism that displayed astute observational analysis of events and had been replaced by the two or three paragraphs quick take on news, as if people could no longer spare the time for an understanding of what was going on in the world. People had grown, of late, to such a reverence for the on-line words that it bordered on obsession, and the old faculty of disseminating news by newspaper had become atrophied. Today, word of a murder is on-line almost as it is being committed so instantaneous is the news, but the problem is there is no analysis, only the sordid details without any in-depth thought or review of the facts. You meet a man on the train who blurts out that a murder was just committed in Port Elizabeth and there is all the difference in the world between the impression you receive from such a chance communication and that given by a detailed analysis in print with the name, the street, the date and all the facts of the case. People who rely on the internet repeat all sorts of tales, far too many of them false; newspapers, unlike the internet, do not print accounts of murders that have not been committed, and when it comes to politics, people have no exposure to anything but their own particular take on things, as they only seek out that which supports their belief system.

Real person-to-person communication Lynton thought was a rarity in today's world, as she gazed about the coach and noticed nearly everyone with cell-phones in their hands, ignoring people for the embrace of technology that was isolating the human race from one another, as each person lived in their own world with less and less human contact, even when others were all around them. Technology was supposed to build bridges between people, but, in reality, it had erected barriers. She sighed, put her cell phone away and looked out the window, taking in the beauty of South Africa, a nation that once seethed with bigotry but now embraced reconciliation and a new hope in a racially harmonious society.

LYNTON AND THE STELLENBOSCH TERROR

She thought of the reverence she had for the printed word, and how that printed word had made her write Wayne Frye years ago and thank him for the magnificent book she had read entitled *When Jesus Came to Jersey as the Son of Thunder*, which had opened her eyes to the tyranny of religion that had been put into the hands of those who distorted everything Jesus stood for. She never received a reply, as obviously, his volume of fan mail far exceeded his ability to respond to everyone. Then, when she was singing in a Vancouver casino, a movie producer mutual friend who had utilized the singing, dancing and acting talents of Lynton in a movie, made an introduction that lit a fuse neither Lynton nor Wayne could put out. Their May-December romance blossomed and grew, despite Wayne's protestations that their age difference was simply too great. As always with the dynamic dynamo, she got her way through the skilful art of the tease and her refusal to allow Wayne to escape her web of love that had entangled him forever in her magnificent and glorious embrace of the positive rather than the negative. She saw age as just a number and told him that she could die of a heart attack; get run over crossing the street or perhaps be killed in one of those obscene drone strikes conducted by the USA all over the world that was constantly killing innocent civilians. Her badgering that he must stop the nonsense about age difference finally broke his will, and he no longer let that barrier be erected. Like that ridiculous wall between the USA and Mexico that was the mainstay that got Donald Trump elected to the U.S. Presidency, she saw the stupidity of building walls when what the world needed was bridges, and she wanted to build a bridge of love between her and Wayne. That was the beauty of the Lynton Viñas, who refused to erect barriers to hope and love.

It is true that in today's technologically driven absurd reporting, vain rumours and fantastic tales are so widely believed by a literally ignorant public that it is fatal to the credit of any stray mutterings that pass as news. People have been taken in by politicians who only serve their own interests and by false preachers of God's word who pile up personal riches as the ignorant flood the collection plates with donations. How ironic that the poor are willing to part with their money, so those who preach about the non-materialistic Jesus, can live in luxurious splendour.

People fall for the false notion that there is some evil lurking out there just waiting to pounce on the unsuspecting. That had been evident when Americans foolishly elected a narcissistic, ignorant, border-line psychopath in 2016 to the presidency. Appealing to people's bigotry and fears was a ticket into the White House for Donald Trump. Ironically, most Americans were not evil, but were far too ill-informed to realize the folly of electing a bombastic, buffoonish man to an office that he would use to enrich and aggrandize himself at their expense. However, the penchant for electing anti-intellectual fools to the office was more the norm than the exception, as another scion of wealth, who like Trump, inherited his privilege, George W. Bush, was elected twice by those who could not see they were voting against their own self-interest. Americans were the laughing stock of the world. Still, they paraded around waving flags, proclaiming their greatness and praising Jesus, while ignoring the fact they were probably living in the most oppressive democracy on the planet. They had been brainwashed and propagandized into subservience to a belief in their superiority which was actually inferiority. Thus, Lynton's own Wayne had left that nation and embraced real freedom in Canada, where the people were more compassionate and willing to lend a helping hand to the downtrodden.

As Lynton was reflecting on all Wayne had taught her about the manipulated gullible Americans, instinct made her reach down and pick up her phone. She went to the South African News Network, almost from force-of-habit, as she was a voracious consumer of news. What she saw was not particularly interesting as she scanned up and down, then her eyes focused in on a news story about an old hotel that had been a place of horror since the early 1900's, as every guest assigned the room 227 would usually come screaming from it, saying there was something terrible that was there, something hideous, something evil. Lynton grinned, thinking to herself that it was of no interest to her. She was on a relaxing journey, not on another demon hunting adventure.

A very tall, slender, handsome young man took a seat across from her and smiled. His eyes were focused directly on her, but she had no time or interest in other men, as, although her husband was certainly no longer considered handsome, he was, to her, the only man in whom she had a romantic interest.

The gentlemen, like every man, could not take his eyes off Lynton. She was used to stares and looked at them as nothing more than the superficially prurient interest of men who were always thinking with their libidos, rather than their brains. Yet, she remembered how Wayne had always told her to be cordial to everyone, so a courteous smile was returned. It was a gesture she would regret. The man got up, sauntered over to the seat where she was sitting, which was facing him, and sat down beside her. He turned toward her and said, "I could not help as I walked by you before taking a seat, not only how beautiful you are, but how you were reading about the Stellenbosch terror."

Lynton, not wanting to be rude, but preferring to avoid discussion if at all possible, replied, "No, I did not read the article, just glanced at the headline. I have no interest in the story or in talking with anyone. You see, I have had a harrowing experience in the Karoo Escarpment, and I am simply taking this train ride for relaxation, peace and quiet."

"Oh, please pardon me madam. I am sorry to interrupt your quiet train ride, but I immediately recognized you, recognized you from that great adventure that was in the newspaper. You and the Lord of the Karoo, Barbizon, are well known even outside the Karoo Escarpment area."

LYNTON AND THE STELLENBOSCH TERROR

Sighing, Lynton replied. "I do not mean to be rude, but I am on a brief respite from that adventure, and the one I had before that when we were able to keep the old South African atomic bombs out of the hands of a terrorist. I am exhausted from all the turmoil, the drama and adventure that frankly I simply do not need in my life anymore."

"Yes, I can appreciate that," he replied in a sombre, deeply earnest tone. "Someone like you, no doubt, has so many people begging for your assistance."

Again sighing, she said, "No one ever has to beg, I am more than willing to help those who are overwhelmed with mystery and intrigue in lives that are far too often thrown asunder by the supernatural or the natural inclination of some people to promulgate the evil of a world where the few rule with impunity over the many. I appreciate your recognition of me. It is flattering, but frankly and in sincere, heartfelt honesty, I have come to find my modest fame and apparent popularity somewhat disconcerting on far too many occasions."

The man got up, started to walk away, but stood and looked back as he said, "I understand. I shall not bother you with tales of the Stellenbosch terror then. It is a mystery that has gone unsolved for around one-hundred years, and, will unfortunately, go on unsolved for maybe a hundred years more. That article is just a salacious attempt to once again drag up that which infuriates the owners of the hotel, of which I am one, my mother being the other. We are sick of the publicity which gets us guests for awhile, but then eventually leads to what is a nightmare of unwanted publicity about the terror in that accursed room. The Stellenbosch Inn is our livelihood, and if it were not for the pub within it, we would be destitute."

She was in trouble now. She told herself not to do it, not to go against her husband's wishes, but her natural curiosity could not be constrained. She said, "I know I will regret this, but sit back down, and tell me of this terror in the hotel."

J. WAYNE FRYE

LYNTON AND THE STELLENBOSCH TERROR

Thus began another Lynton adventure, one that would make most of her past encounters with the supernatural seem like child's play, as this time she would face off against an entity that was as sinister as any she had ever encountered. She was about to prepare for the coming terror.

Lynton Viñas – Renowned Demon Fighter

Steam train Lynton took to Stellenbosch

where she listened to

tales of the Stellenbosch Terror.

Chapter 2

They Fear Thinkers

Where had been an unholy thing,

For an unholy haunting it resided,

Scraping with cold skeleton hands.

The feeble ashes of feeble breath

Blew about to extinguish the flame,

Which was a mockery not lifted up.

Viewer eyes scared; the evil beheld.

This demonic thing long ago died.

Famine of soul it was in a void.

The evil was piled in a lump,

LYNTON AND THE STELLENBOSCH TERROR

Season-less, dearth of love, lifeless,
A pile of death as hard as clay.
The rivers, lakes and oceans stood still,
And nothing stirred within silent depths;
The deathly smell of decay the room did fill.
The abyss of hell waited without a surge.
Thing so long dead should be in a grave,
Light could not penetrate the darkness.
No hope was in the dank, stagnant air,
And the room embraced this darkness.

The stranger introduced himself as Adam Kruger, and Lynton, not wanting to get involved in another adventure, but still immensely curious, as was natural for her, said, "So, I am not about to get involved in another battle with an assumed demon, but I must voice some interest in what you call the Stellenbosch terror. Perhaps you could provide a few details."

"Details you want my dear Ms. Viñas? Oh my little demon fighter, there are such incredible tales that even someone as skilled and informed as you are would question the veracity of a person describing what has occurred all these years in Stellenbosch."

"Do not credit me with too much in the battle against demons. Although I have seen and heard things that make the flesh crawl, I sometimes doubt my own eyes and ears. However, do tell me about his thing you call a terror, so that I may accumulate some knowledge of that which apparently hovers about Stellenbosch, as I have never been there and want to know all I can."

"You see, the terror is sometimes confined. Yet, it manifests itself all about the town but prefers the isolation of that infernal hotel room. But, the containment is only temporary at best, for periodically it escapes the confines of those four walls and walks among the people, bringing its evil to so many. I shall share with you the very beginning of the terror." And thus began the tale.

"One night in July, about 100 years ago, a sturdy-looking fellow left town after a night of private drinking in room 227 with a university teacher from Cape Town. His cottage was five or six kilometres away, upon the banks of the Eerste River. The ground was barren and covered with loose dirt, which in many places had drifted into heaps, filtering onto the compacted road and making it slippery in spots, impeding the progress of his old horse and buggy making its way toward his cottage. Still, nature looked very beautiful, and the heart of the rustic area was touched by the sweet peacefulness of the scene. The moon shed its soft silvery light into the long silent valley, stretching away until its virgin paleness mingled with the shadows and the darkness of the distant water fall beyond the bend in the river."

"All was still, save the whistling wind rustling gently through the frosted branches of the leafless trees by the roadside, and a shaking down upon the wayfarer of a miniature shower of drifting mist. This place was always full of mirth and music in the summer time, but in the winter, the cold of Southern Africa could bite to the bone and the tourists had no interest in this place at that time. On rare occasions, some light snow would fall on the little houses, half-hidden by the towering mountain that soared skyward. The valley seemed at peace as all was quiet and serene. Still, there was something foreboding in the air."

It was difficult for Adam to keep his eyes off Lynton, whose skin resembled a soft, smooth pomegranate glistening in the sun, eyes a dark shade of brown twinkling with mischievousness and obsidian hair like dark brown leaves fluttering in the autumn breeze. The way her long lashes flicked in unison and the way her full, thick lips curled into a seductive grin displaying glistening white teeth made Adam take a deep breath to get his mind back on the tale he was sharing. He had to be forgiven his fascination, because such fascination was inevitable once a man looked upon her, taking in those delightfully muscular calves that had been honed to perfection from years as a professional dancer. She kept you still and mesmerized to the point you were lost in an obsessive trance, and men; in particular, would get that tingle that reminded them that this was an extraordinary woman. In fact, men usually came to the realization this was a succubus of desire, who was beautiful, alluring, captivating and a little bit dangerous.

Adam continued his story. "Harold was by no means a timid or nervous being, but there was a nameless something in the deathly silence that night which hung in the crisp air. He earnestly wished himself safely across the little bridge over the narrow part of the river; but he was yet some distance from it when his pocket watch chimes signalled midnight. Almost immediately after the last stroke of twelve had broken the silence, a cloud passed over the face of the moon, and comparative darkness enveloped the scene. The wind, which before had been fairly gentle with a slight whispering, began to howl amid the boughs and branches of the waving trees, and the cold air slapped Harold's face."

Lynton had to admit he was a fantastic story teller, as he kept her on the edge of her seat with anticipation at what was coming next. He, sensing her interest, continued in earnest. "He had already begun to fancy that he could distinguish in the howling of the wind and the creaking of the boughs unearthly manifestations about; but as he approached the dreaded bridge, his courage almost entirely failed him, and it required a great effort to keep from turning his buggy around and galloping rapidly back to town. It struck him, however, that he had come a long distance and that if he did go back people might laugh at him for being afraid to go home. He thought that if he could only cross the bridge he would be safe, free from whatever there was out there waiting in the wind. Yes, whatever it was would lose its power once he crossed the bridge. Influenced by this thought, yet with his knees knocking under him, he pushed forward with more assured boldness, and he had almost reached the bridge when he heard the noise of shuffling feet in the dirt, and became conscious of the presence of a ghastly thing he was unable to see. Suddenly a moaning, horrendously sad howl in the wind brought him to a stop, and, with his heart throbbing loudly enough to be heard, he gazed fixedly into the darkness. There was nothing to be perceived, but the bridge in the near distance."

"He might have stayed there until daylight had not another cry in the wind, louder and even more unearthly and horrible than the preceding one, called him from his motionless-like trance. No sooner had this second howling died away than, impelled by an irresistible impulse, he stepped down from the buggy and stood there staring into the darkness to his left. Taking the reins of the horse, he moved forward on foot, pulling the horse and buggy behind him. He was more curious than scared now, so he moved in the direction whence the howling had come. At that moment the moon burst forth from behind the clouds, which had for some time obscured the light, and the rays fell upon the road, with its half-hidden cart-tracks winding away into the dim distance; and in the very centre of the bridge he beheld a hideous figure with black shaggy hide, and huge eyes closely resembling orbs of misery. He sensed this evil looking thing was an ambassador of death, his death. It hovered in the middle of the bridge."

Lynton uncrossed her gorgeous legs and for a second, Adam paused, looking at her lustfully, letting his mind revel in the glory of her glistening brownness. His eyes were drawn to her now slightly parted legs, but his gaze moved up to her majestically pure breathing that accentuated her magnificently formed shapely orb like breasts. Adam did not believe in God, but he thought that if he did, then this woman would be his masterpiece.

Lynton was used to the attention, but sometimes it was annoying. She smiled and said, as he stared at her breasts, "My dear Adam, I am flattered you find me interesting, but your story cannot be finished by staring at that which is off-limits. Why not continue your story."

"I am so sorry, Ms. Viñas, I do not mean to be rude, but I am not used to seeing such a beautiful woman."

"Tell you what," replied a grinning Lynton, "You finish the tale, and I'll sit here and let you stare at me all you want. Please, you have piqued my interest."

Struggling to regain his composure, Adam said, "I am again so sorry. I do not intend to be rude."

Lynton, more serious now, said, "You will only be rude of you do not continue with your tale."

"Yes, of course I will continue. Anyway, Harold was not as frightened now, as at least what he had heard was there for him to see. Without any consciousness of what he was doing, he dropped the horse's reins and acting as though under the sway of a strange and irresistibly mesmerizing influence, he stepped towards the bridge; but no sooner did he stir than the frightful thing in front of him, with a motion that was not walking, but rather a sort of heavy gliding, moved also, slowly retreating, pausing when he paused, and always keeping its sorrowful eyes fixed upon his face. Slowly he crossed the river, but gradually his steps grew more and more rapid, until he broke into a run. Suddenly a faint knowledge of the horrible nature of his position dawned upon him. A little cottage stood by the roadside and from one of its chamber-windows, very near to the ground, a dim light shone. Influenced by a sudden feeling of companionship, Adam tried to cry out, but his tongue could not move in his parched mouth, and suddenly the light in the cottage went out, and he never felt so alone and helpless. Still that infernal thing kept gliding backwards. Harold broke into a run, assuming he could skirt around it. The sorrowful red eyes of the abominable thing seemed to be pleading, staring directly at him. There appeared to be urgency in those eyes, almost as if whatever it was impeding his progress forward wanted to communicate something, but what could a horrible apparition like that evil-appearing thing before him want to communicate. He reflected back on his drinking buddy, the teacher from the university who had told him not to go home, not to tempt fate that night, because something wicked was afoot."

"He stumbled over a stone on the road. Overcome by a fear that the ghastly object would seize him, he regained his feet, and, to his intense relief, the horrendous entity was no longer visible. With a sigh of pleasure he sat down upon a heap of broken stones, for his limbs, no longer forced into mechanical movement by the influence of the spectre's presence, refused to bear him further. Bitterly cold as was that night; still, the perspiration stood in beads upon his whitened face, and, with the recollection of those terrible eyes and horrible body strong upon him, he shook and shivered. A strong and burly man, in the very prime of life, he felt as weak as a new born baby. He revived himself and regained his feet, went back to get in the buggy without fear now that the horse would be spooked and resumed his lonely journey, trudging along at a slow gallop."

"Again, the moon disappeared behind a cloud and a keen and cutting blast of wind swept through the scrub forest to his left, where the barren trees were like solemn sentinels upon the entrance to purgatory. There was that mournfully sorrowful moaning again, as if the scrub trees to were withered corpses raised from the grave. There was a lull, and the breeze ceased even to whisper. The silence was more painful than were the noises of mournful moaning, for it filled his heart with forebodings of coming woe. He was gently flicking the reins as he looked to his right at the banks of the river and saw decayed vegetation crawling up the bank, crawling as if it were some primal evil working its way from the depths of the dank, dark, slow moving river that was hugging the terror of the moment."

"Then, he heard a murmuring voice, and with a sinking feeling, he sensed the coming appearance of the ghastly figure. He had not to wait long, for as he reached the curve in the road, once more he saw, in the centre of the road right before him, the same terrible evil entity in a dark cloak with a hood on its head, and those eyes, those sorrowful red eyes that were burning as if projecting the misery of the grave. He was impelled forward, and once more the strange backward procession commenced, the gliding, not walking, rear movement. The ghastly apparition put out its two boney hands and made a stopping motion as if urging, no pleading with him to halt, but whatever the thing was it apparently did not have the power to stop him."

"Harold was now in a desperate mode. He had to get home, but this thing kept impeding his progress. Why, he thought, was it apparently keeping him from the warm arms of his wife and child? What did this evil thing want from him? Was it after his soul?"

"His cottage was only a short distance down the road now. The menacing entity slowly moved backwards toward his cabin, until it settled in front of the door, as if intending to block him from entering. Then, as he looked into its eyes, gazed upon the high cheek bones, he felt that he knew this thing. There was a familiarity to it."

"Harold climbed down from the buggy. He stood for a few seconds watching the thing hovering there in front of the door. He seemed to be in a trance, moving slowly toward the horribly menacing entity. As he neared it, in a fit of wild desperation, he struck at it, but his hand banged against the oak of the door as it was apparently transparent, and, as the spectre fluttered away, he managed to somehow open the door and fall into the cabin."

"Disturbed by the noise of the fall, Harold's wife arose from bed, ran into the entryway and drew him into the cottage, but for some hours he was unable to tell the story of his terrible journey. When he had told of his horrible experience, a deep gloom fell over the woman's features, for she well knew that the ghastly visit portended ill-fortune for them. The dread of uncertainty over what lay ahead did not continue long, however, for on the third day from that upon which Harold had reached his home, his only child, a mere ten years old was brought to the cottage by neighbours apparently drowned in an accident, but drained of all blood; and after attending the child's funeral,

Harold's wife sickened from a mysterious loss of blood, and within a few weeks she too was dispatched into eternity. These things, together with the dreadful experience of that journey, so affected Harold that he lost his sanity. Few believed him when he recounted tales of that terrible night. It was laughed off as the ravings of a crazy man, who eventually was taken away to die as a screaming lunatic in an insane asylum."

Lynton sighed, and somewhat disappointed, said, "But what does this have to do with what is in that room at the hotel?"

"That you will hear of eventually, because I am not finished, yet. There is more, much more to the tale of woe. This all happened around 1918, but then, after that there were others at regular intervals who experienced similar occurrences, the most unusual being when my great grandparents, who operated the very inn where Harold had been drinking on that faithful night, remodelled it into a place of ornate beauty, though a bit pedestrian for any of the upper class. In that place, my grandmother was born and it was she who, as a young girl growing up in the hotel, heard of tales about the strange occurrences that had apparently driven Harold mad. Only a few believed in what he had seen, but in my grandmother's ninth year, she was plying the hallways of the great chateau, riding on her tricycle to and fro with wild abandon. Then it happened for the first time."

Lynton interrupted. "She saw the same entity that was described by Harold."

"Yes, how did you know?"

With a tinge of exasperation, Lynton replied, "She had been told the story by other children. It is not unusual for children to imagine things at that age, especially when they have been fed a steady diet of horror stories. Where do you think nightmares come from? In the Philippines, as children, we are told of Aswangs, and in this modern world a whopping 60% of Filipinos believe in this vampire-like creature. Why do you think the church insists on young people going to Sunday School? It is about getting fertile, young, pliable, untapped minds and plying them with stories of devils, demons and a place called hell where the bad will burn and only the power of God can cast out these evil entities. This is the way of a world where there are always those who do not want thinkers. They fear thinkers."

Chapter 3

Stellenbosch Terror Come to do Its Mischief

Doors open and close by themselves,

As the dead prance all about.

Creepy moans from a closet

Make the mind numb.

Oh, it will come; it will come.

Dance a waltz of death evil spirit.

It wants to open the gates to hell,

Where torment eternally abides.

From the body a soul it wants to sever.

The evil spirit will bring you pain forever.

LYNTON AND THE STELLENBOSCH TERROR

Lynton was now growing weary of what she was beginning to see as nothing more than a man's attempt to enthral her, and make her his play thing for a day. She had seen it far too often.

"My dear Adam, I thank you for spinning a good yarn, but frankly I am not amused. I came on the train ride for some rest after a hair-raising adventure in the Karoo. Surely, you can comprehend my desire for some relaxation. I do not wish to be rude, but, alas, you are obviously romantically interested in me," and then she extended her left hand, displaying a wedding ring. "As you can see, I am married, and if you had read the books about me, as you indicated you had, then you would know that I am a loyal wife, not given to flights of fancy with other men."

Almost apologetically, Adam replied, "My dear Ms. Viñas, I am, as any normal man would be, titillated by your beauty I admit. However, I assure you that my intentions are honourable. Although if offered, I would certainly partake of pleasures of the flesh with you, I am not here to make an attempt at anything nefarious. I am just interested in perhaps having you, since you are skilled at dealing with so-called demons, take a look at our hotel and give us your opinion."

"O.K., I am sorry if I appeared rude. It is not my normal habit to exhibit rudeness. Perhaps you should go on then. Tell me about what your grandmother saw."

"Thank you, I shall endeavour to not be overly demonstrative in my perusal of your magnificent womanly assets, but surely, you are used to the fascination of men?"

Smiling, almost to the point of laughing, Lynton said, "Men are such ninnies. None of you think with your heads. Your brains seem to be a bit lower down, and they appear to have grey matter that percolates with but one thought." Then, she did laugh out loud, and so did he, as now there was a developing simpatico.

As they shared a laugh, the dining car waiter strolled by and Adam asked if Lynton would like a drink. She replied that a tea would be nice. Thus, they sat for awhile, sipping tea together and not even mentioning the tales of spirits. Lynton sensed that he was now less amorously inclined, as she was good at dulling the ardour of men as well as stimulating it. She felt more comfortable with him and finally said, "Alright, now tell me about what your grandmother saw."

"Well, as she was peddling down the hallway, she almost froze as she noticed room 227 had a shadow hanging over the door, which floated back in the depth of its arched recess, like an unfathomable eye under a frowning brow. The room doors in the inn are wide and paneled, and a heavy, thick, large intricately carved door knob, seemed to be turning on its own. My grandmother was frozen still, but managed to look back over her shoulder at the dark staircase behind her. The other doors lining the hallway were dark also; but one other was with a difference. The top of the landing had a room door immediately to the right that was lightest of all, because of the skylight; and perhaps it was largely by reason of contrast that its aforementioned doorway gloomed so black and forbidding. All the doors down the hallway all opened and then slammed shut, all but that one, the door with the shadow above it. She felt compelled to enter room 227. It was as if she was hypnotized. She climbed off her tricycle and slowly moved toward the door. This was a room that had rarely been rented, because my great grandmother, no matter how hard she tried, could never get an odious smell from the room. She had said that it smelled like the rotting flesh of some carcass. She used every cleaning method know at the time, but the smell still lingered. And as my grandmother approached that door it slowly opened. Inside, she saw darkness so black it was as if she could have cut it with a knife. She began to feel as if she was no longer walking, but floating steadily forward toward that abominable room. Suddenly, a couple came up the stairs, stepped onto the landing and turned down the hallway. The door to the room closed with a thud, which sounded like the closing of a tomb. My grandmother seemed to come out of her trance as the giggling couple continued down the hallway. For years, my grandmother never revealed the experience, and she avoided the second floor."

Adam stood for awhile to stretch his legs, sat back down and continued. "Long even before the last tenant had occupied it, the room had been regarded with fear and aversion by almost everyone. Even when it was not rented, people staying on the second floor would say they heard strange noises emanating from the room, and there was a growing sense, a premonition if you will, that made my grandmother think that something extremely bad was going to happen, and it did. It did with a wild, unnerving, mind-boggling appearance of an apparition one day in May of 1938."

"The chateau was so old that it had endured many Stellenbosch hardships over the years, and somehow emerged in tack, having even survived a fire in 1933 that nearly destroyed the whole town. Still, the old place rose proud, almost noble in appearance, but the locals, who would visit the pub portion of the hotel with a degree of regularity that has kept it operating all these years, simply would not stay the night, because the cleaning crew had relayed stories about cold spots in the second floor hallway and eerie moaning coming from room 227."

"For years the room had not even been entered into, but my grandmother was a gregarious child and teenager, and she was extremely curious. Yet, she feared going onto that second floor. A few years went by and the fear of that room did not diminish in intensity. Finally, she made a trip to the town library to research the history of the chateau, and maybe ferret out some details that might satisfy her curiosity. She discovered that Harold had spent, because of inclement weather, the previous night in town before his trip back to his cottage. He stayed at the château owned by my great grandparents."

Lynton interrupted. "And he stayed in room 227?"

"Yes, and he awakened the entire place in the middle of the night with screams of horror. He was shivering with fear."

Interrupting, Lynton said, "And he was convinced it was a nightmare, a nightmare in which he saw a thin, almost skeleton-like cloaked figure with deep recessed, pleading eyes that were fiery red?"

"Yes, it was exactly as you say."

"Alas, it was the same figure he would see on the bridge and in front of his cottage door," interjected Lynton.

"Of course, yes, and after Harold's fright there and the subsequent death of his child and his wife, as well as his commitment to an asylum, nobody would go into the room, for there was an odious smell there, one of decaying flesh. All this was discovered at the library's archives in notes my grandmother found in an old diary kept by a former maid at the château. The furniture was taken out of the room, sold and the room locked for years. Then, in the spring of 1946, my great grandparents died, leaving the hotel to my grandmother who was only 25. When one is twenty-five, healthy, hungry and modestly trying to find your way in the world, one is less likely to be frightened by a room, even though you have had some weird experiences related to it. My grandmother put the past behind her, and she, believe it or not, took up residence in the room, as she decided to endure the smell in order to be able to rent the other rooms for needed revenue, as she had an affair with a married man and wound up with my mother as a result. At this time, my grandmother took up painting, partly because she thought the smell of paints would mask the smell of the room. It did, for the most part."

"She resided there with my mother for many years and there was nothing out of the ordinary materialized, only the occasional intense smell. When my mother was seven, my grandmother gave her a room next door that she had put a play area in, thus the two were separated at night while sleeping. It seemed that my grandmother's fears of the room were nothing more than childhood fantasies and peacefulness prevailed."

"As time went on, the huge room was altered time and again, even adding another room from the immenseness that made my grandmother think it made more sense to make it into sort of an apartment, because of its size. One day my grandmother came up from downstairs, and felt uneasiness, and that feeling from childhood crept back over her. As she looked down the hallway from the landing on the stairs where she stoically stood, the dark shadow above the door, after all these years, was there again. Still, she was a mature woman now, and would not be overwhelmed by what she had grown to consider nonsensical farce."

"She entered the room without hesitation, walked across to the window facing the street and threw it open. The chimneys and roofs of many houses straggled before her, and she observed the twin steeples of the church across the street and to her right. As she stood there, darkness descended upon those steeples, a huge cloud covering the peaks of them as a lighting bolt flashed."

"At the very moment the lighting bolt flashed across the sky, the unpleasant smell came about, penetrating her nostrils. Oh, and there was a feeling there too, a feeling that invaded all the senses. Still, my grandmother thought, as a grown woman, this was nothing but the reflection upon a childhood fantasy of fear. It was with something of amused bravado that she feared not that which she had once considered a haunted room; for, now she readily convinced herself that this disgust and dislike while in the room were the result of imagination and nothing more. She resolved to face the matter with a resolute mind. An idea then began to germinate. There had been rumours about this room, and she fancied herself a fairly skilled writer, so she postulated a newspaper or magazine in Cape Town might actually be interested in a well-crafted article about a haunted room. So, she considered the room a boon to her financial status as well as something that was a high old adventure. To do the article right, she should return to the library for more research."

"No, she thought, there was nothing to be gained by more boring research. She would make up things to heighten the readability of the piece. The window remained wide open and the paints were all opened, but it was still there, that depressing, choking, putrid smell, something that entered the consciousness and rattled the brain. But she could give no proper attention to any work, as she felt there was a presence there as she kept glancing about the room more than once yielding to a childish impulse to look inside the closet with a closed door that was creepily now seeming to pulsate. She laughed at herself for being so childish. She averted looking at the closet door. Suddenly, as she was sitting in a caned back chair, she realized she had pushed it all the way to the far wall across the room. She could now take the whole room into view. There was darkness outside that window as a sunny day had become sullenly overcast. She looked at the huge dagger-like letter opener on the desk to her right. It was a pointed, deadly murderous weapon she thought."

Lynton was thinking too, thinking this man was in love with his story-telling ability. He was relishing how he was enthralling her with his tale. Still, she had to admit that she was actually immensely interested. It had genuinely captivated her and piqued her sense of curiosity.

"As my grandmother gazed at that letter opener the rest of the room grew dim, but then she saw the closet doorknob turning and under the threshold a dark cloud crept out across the floor. With a sudden clang, the heavy bells of the church aroused her, and she shook her head violently as if trying to release the cobwebs that were clouding her brain with fantasy."

"There lay the dagger-like letter opener on the table, almost glowing with murderous intent, seeming to lure her toward the table to pick it up. She fought the urge by closing her eyes. When she opened them again, her chair, which had been back against the wall, was now some six or seven feet forward, close by the table; clearly, she must have drawn it forward without an observable reason. That could be the only explanation. She was next to that dagger-like letter opener now. She was cold, almost shivering. She reached for the dagger, grabbed it and held it up before herself, feeling an urge to plunge it into her heart. She pulled open the desk drawer, flung it in and slammed the drawer shut. She felt as if she had been drugged, but somehow managed to pull herself up from the chair, moved ever so slowly toward the door, but had to fight an unseen force that appeared to be holding her, making each step she took an arduous exercise in determination to get out of that room. Finally, she reached the door and it took great effort to turn the knob and an even greater effort to push the door open. She pushed, shoved, huffed and puffed until she finally got it open enough to wedge her way out of the room into the hallway."

Lynton, a woman of infinite patience wondered where all this was leading. Why was he telling the story in such an infernal rambling fashion, rather than getting to the point. Still, she could not but grow desirous to hear more.

He continued. "She went slowly downstairs and out into the streets. She grew ashamed of herself, for as she sucked in the fresh air she had to admit she feared that room. She knew there was a presence there, something not human. She was breathing heavily, still engrossed with fear. Whatever was in that room had immense power, power so immense that few people were able to resist it."

"As she walked in the darkness with the street lamps glittering in the misty night air, she knew that there was going to be hell in that hotel, a hell unleashed by an unknown entity, but she also knew that it was that entity encountered by Harold Minter so many years before, an entity that drove him insane. Was it going to do that to her as well? Or would it do worse?"

"She became convinced that the hotel was indeed haunted, if by nothing else, by a spirit of fear within her that was overwhelming. She felt angry at the growing conviction that she had allowed herself to be saddled with fright."

Lynton interjected, "Sometimes I have found that fear is the chief ingredient that allows minds to connect dots that are nothing more than hallucinatory manifestations conjured up by the pliable minds of those who subject themselves to delusional beliefs in demons from hell. But alas, I have interrupted you. Tell me more about your grandmother, because I know she went back into that room, because she was a woman who did not run from fear, but faced it. Am I right?"

Nodding affirmatively, Adam said, "Oh, yes, definitely. She returned that night with the resolve to allow herself no foolish indulgence. She sat there that very night seemingly waiting for something to happen, desirous to confront whatever it was and not cower in fear. My mother was safe in the adjoining room, but she was suffering great consternation, so she could not sleep herself, fearful of what was going on."

"Dazzling sunlight through the window woke my grandmother in the morning and she crawled out of bed groggy, as if she had drunk too much alcohol the night before. She suddenly recalled dreams, horrid dreams of the grave and being in the damp, dark ground. She rubbed her eyes and stared amazedly down at the table. She shuttered at what she saw. There it was, the very dagger-like letter opener she had put in the drawer before."

Lynton leaned slightly forward and said, "Oh my Adam. This shall not end well. I can sense it."

"My mother came in," offered Adam, "and she could see my grandmother shivering in fear. She walked swiftly to her side, reached up to clasp her hands and asked her what was wrong, and in near shock, my grandmother shared all that had transpired the day before and how she was now fearful of the intent of whatever evil entity had materialized from the past and was now renewing its haunting."

"My mother tried unsuccessfully to console her. She walked over and put the letter opener back in the drawer. My mother helped my grandmother dress, and they went downstairs. As they were having breakfast, my grandmother excused herself to go back upstairs and get her jacket as she complained of being chilled. To this day, my mother blames herself for letting her go back up to that infernal room alone."

Lynton let a scowl of sorrow crease across her lips, as she said, "Your mother went back up and found her dead."

"Yes my dear Lynton. She was sitting on the floor, back against the bed, a look of terror burned onto her face, eyes bulging, a steady stream of blood oozing from the fatal wound. The strange thing is she had two piercings in her heart. Just tiny little wounds and all the blood had been drained from her lifeless body. She was pale with that horrible look of fear burned into her eyes."

Head bowed and tears in his eyes, Adam's cracking voice uttered words that had pieced Lynton's psyche, "It was the Stellenbosch terror come to do its mischief."

Chapter 4

A Reign of Terror

Lynton on to Stellenbosch in the dark fall;

There where a ghost in evil will stall,

And in the twilight wait for what will come.

The leaves will whisper there of her, and some,

Like flying words, will strike Lynton as they fall;

But go, and if you listen the ghost will call.

Go to the dark place Lynton my sweet,

And this ghost try to boldly defeat.

No, there is not a dawn in dark skies

LYNTON AND THE STELLENBOSCH TERROR

To pierce the fire burning in her eyes;
But there, where glooms are gathering,
Dark will come determined and smothering:
Good is slain with every dark leaf that flies,
And hell embraces the light that it defies.
Go to the dark place Lynton my sweet,
And this ghost try to boldly defeat.

Out of a grave it comes to tell her this.
Out of a grave it comes to plant death's kiss.
It places flames upon her forehead with a glow
That blinds her to the way that she must go.
Yes, there is evil about in that room,
Where dear Lynton could meet her doom.
Go to the dark place Lynton my sweet,
And this ghost try to boldly defeat.

There is no attempt for the spectre to stall,
As the crimson leaves fall upon doom's wall.
Go, for the winds are tearing them away,
Nor think to riddle the dead words they say,
Nor any more to feel them as they fall.

J. WAYNE FRYE

LYNTON AND THE STELLENBOSCH TERROR

Can't you hear that ghostly spectre call?
Go to the dark place Lynton my sweet,
And this ghost try to boldly defeat.

Stellenbosch is a city of around 150,000, but at its heart, it is a small town, and when Adam's mother greeted him at the station, she was pleased to know he had met up with the famous demon fighter from the Philippines, who was now also famous in South Africa after her two adventures in the Karoo. When he told her that she would look into the ghostly goings-on at their inn, she gushed with excitement, but no real surprise.

The town's oak-shaded streets were lined with cafes, boutiques and art galleries. Cape Dutch architecture gave it an ancient feel, and as Lynton sat in the back of Adam's car, his mother, Cecile, kept looking back at her and commenting on how beautiful she was. Embarrassed, Lynton said, "I appreciate the compliment, but believe me, I know that any woman who is called beautiful should break her mirror at an early age, because it is a transitory state that, if you let capture your soul, will destroy any real beauty you have, because, in most cases, beautiful women are disappointing."

Cecile was impressed with Lynton's depth of wisdom, and as they approached the hotel, she looked over the seat back as they pulled up at the inn on the outskirts of town, and said, "Fortunately, we are the same size it appears. I know you have no clothes with you, so please, once you get settled in, come to my room and you can wear whatever clothes of mine you like."

Lynton, to Cecile's surprise said, "I want to stay in Room 227, if possible. Are you still in that room?"

"No, when my mother died in that room, I took the quarters downstairs. Adam and I live there, have for 37 years now. Are you sure you want to stay in 227?"

"I am very sure, yes."

The door to 227 begrudgingly creaked open and a musty, dank odour permeated Lynton's nostrils. The room embraced deadly silence except for the intermittent sound of cars on the street outside.

LYNTON AND THE STELLENBOSCH TERROR

Lynton quietly entered the living room. Windows covered with brocade curtains still let the shimmering calm light struggle to penetrate the darkness in thin threaded rays. Sharp shadows roamed around the room. The sofa and chairs had deep grooves on them where people had sat. Lynton walked over to the sofa and felt the indentation. It was warm. Picture frames were slightly askew. A misplaced grand bookcase stood in one corner. Lynton traced her right hand fingers over the tops of several books. There was no dust. Looking at Cecile she said, "And no one has been in this room for how long?"

Adam and Cecile looked at one another and in unison said, "Ages."

"Then a ghost has been sitting on the sofa, and apparently has dusted off the books as well. Perhaps we have a clean-freak scholarly ghost on our hands, who enjoys a good read."

Lynton approached the desk where the dagger-like letter opener had lain. Looking down at the desk, she said, "And I suppose the police still have the letter-opener your mother used to kill herself all those years ago?"

Cecile, a sad tone to her voice, replied, "They did, but it disappeared from the evidence locker maybe 20 years ago."

Lynton opened the drawer, reached in it and pulled out an ornate letter opener with Egyptian hieroglyphics on it. Holding it up, she asked if it was the letter opener used to end her mother's life.

Aghast that it was there, Cecile and her son took deep breaths. Adam said, "I, I, I, why that is it, yes, but how?"

Lynton, gently placing the letter opener on the table, replied, "A bit unusual to say the least isn't it?"

Tired from her journey, Lynton retired unafraid in the room and slept through the night without incident. She got up early, and walked into the hallway on her way to breakfast. She met Adam just as he was coming down the hallway. He smiled and jocularly asked if she had seen any ghosts?

LYNTON AND THE STELLENBOSCH TERROR

Smiling back, she replied, "Yes, the ghost of intense hunger. I certainly hope you have a skilled chef in your restaurant."

An older man came out of the room two doors down from 227 and greeted Lynton with a nod, but no words, as he hurriedly brushed past her with no acknowledgement of Adam and seemingly leaped down the stairs. Lynton shared a leisurely breakfast with other guests, then rose from the table and announced to Adam and his mother that she was going for a stroll.

Stellenbosch is in a valley, surrounded by mountains that accentuate the beauty of a peaceful, serene place that is seemingly lost in time. The normal hustle and bustle of the city appeared muted here, almost as even the automobiles and buses puttered about with muffled sounds. Lynton stopped to peer into a shop window and observed her reflection in it, seeing herself as worn and haggard from what had apparently been a restless night, despite her lack of ability to recall any details of her sleep that, based upon her appearance, had been less than peaceful. Her haggard look troubled her and into that furtive, knowledgeable mind flashed a remembrance of an old legend about a person who when looking in any mirror, never saw his own face, but the face of a demon. She felt that way this morning, as if she were looking at something other than her normal reflection. She felt incredibly tired.

As she turned to walk back to the inn, she heard a car radio break through the near silence with mention of a murder the night before, a heinous act where someone had been killed near the Stellenbosch Inn.

Lynton made her way to a newsstand and bought a paper. Scanning the story of the murder, it was apparent someone had been killed in a very unusual manner. The individual was found with an intense look of fright on his face, and preliminary reports indicated he appeared to have been literally frightened to death. Then how was it judged to be murder? Reading further, she found there were two slight piercing insertions in what was a wound to his heart. A small piercing instrument had been used, something akin to a letter opener. The body was drained of blood.

Chills went up Lynton's spine as she made haste toward the Stellenbosch Inn. She, upon entering the lobby, found Adam and his mother standing by the entrance, waiting for her arrival. She said, "I know all about it, and the fact that he was stabbed with an instrument similar to a letter opener. Have you examined the room for it yet?"

Adam replied, "We were waiting for you."

The three of them went upstairs, and there it was. The letter opener was on the table, sharp edge pointing away from the three. Warning them not to touch it, she walked into the bathroom and came out with a wash cloth, picked up the letter opener carefully, making sure not to smudge any fingerprints and walked to the window to examine it. Holding it up to the light, she said, "looks like no blood anywhere on it."

"Should we call the police?" asked Adam.

"And tell them what?" replied a puzzled Lynton. "Tell them we suspect a dark cloaked phantom used this letter opener for the coup de grâce?"

Adam, holding the paper now, said, "It was an old homeless man. His name was Drummond. He was just a harmless person who had no family according to the paper. You don't think what we know might help the police?"

"How much assistance do you think telling them all that you have told me will be? I mean they already know the tales I am sure. Assuming they are normal police officers, I am sure they will only laugh at us, scoff at the notion of some fiend from the beyond committing murder."

"I suppose you are right," Adam said as he glanced over at his bewildered mother.

Still reading, Adam offered more information. "There was no robbery; the few Rand the old man possessed remained in his pocket. He must have been attacked on his way home in the early hours of the morning, possibly by a homicidal maniac, and was probably so frightened by whomever approached him that his old heart just gave way, and the article does not postulate on why he was stabbed and his blood drained."

Lynton, from her years of dealing with the supernatural, offered her analysis. "Ritual, it has something to do with a ritual."

Perplexed, Cecile said, "What do you mean a ritual?"

"I am not sure what I mean Cecile. It is just that there are certain elements when you deal with the supernatural, the occult, whatever you want to call it. These elements form a common thread where the belief in rituals can offer either protection or a way of paying homage to an evil entity. Or, maybe the insertion of the object into the heart was nothing but the act of a deranged mind with no known intention other than the unmitigated joy of committing the act itself. I have worked with the famous transgender detective Chablis Louise Chavez on a few occasions, and believe me, there are people in this world who commit heinous acts that you and I would find abhorrent, but for them, it is incredibly satisfying and fulfilling to have the absolute power to decide whether someone lives or dies."

"Then you believe this murder had something to do with whatever is in this room or not?" asked Adam.

"I am not prone to jump to conclusions, Adam. I am assessing and reflecting right now - maybe yes, maybe no."

She then smiled and offered a bit of light heartiness. "Hey, I have a difficult time detecting without a full stomach."

Cecile said, "O.K. Is that a hint for lunch?"

With a slight giggle, Lynton replied, "That's no hint, just a cold hard fact."

After lunch, Lynton surveyed the scene of the old man's death, but saw nothing out of the ordinary. A leisurely dinner and then she retired to room 227. She went to sleep quickly and dreamed, tossing and turning most of the night. Her awaking was abrupt as no bright sun blazed in at the open window to lift her heavy eyelids, and there was no cling and clang of traffic outside. It was pitch black all around her, almost as if she were in a tomb.

She was gasping and staring in the dark, rolling face-downward on the floor, catching her breath in agonized sobs, while through the window from the streets below she heard a clamour of hoarse cries, cries of pursuit and the noise of running men, a shouting and clattering wherein here and there a voice cried out, "The terror, the terror, the terror."

She dragged herself to her feet in the dark, gasping for breath. She was sweating profusely. What was this? Was she still dreaming?

Her legs trembled under her, and sweat beaded up on her brow, despite the cold. She moved toward the window, panting and feeble; and then, as she looked at herself, she realized she was standing there naked, but this was a woman who knew no shame, for she saw the real shame in a world that bowed before convention and embraced judgemental arrogance to point the finger of condemnation rather than embrace humanity with enlightenment. She often thought that clothes were nothing more than an invention of the church to aid corporations by allowing them to make money selling clothing. Hey, the world economy might take a nose dive if people stopped wearing clothes in warm weather. She took a deep breath, standing there looking at the unfolding scene below. The running crowd disappeared, the shouts growing fainter. What had awakened her, and why was she naked, as she had gone to bed in a night gown given her by Cecile that now lay on the bed, and beside it were her other clothes, but she had put them on the sofa before she retired. She walked over and felt her clothes. They were warm, as if someone had them on only a short time ago. "Oh my," she thought, because also there on the desk lay the dagger-like letter opener. Her hands began to tremble. She was breathing heavily now as she glanced into the bathroom mirror and she stared with shivering trepidation, frozen in astonishment. The reflection showed a dark cloaked figure standing behind her, eyes sorrowful like a pleading cry for solace from pain. It was looking at her naked body and there was such intensity pouring forth from the gaze.

She blinked her eyes and the apparition disappeared. She gazed at herself, wondering what caused the commotion outside.

> *Shadowy figures walk the night,*
> *Clearing now within plain sight,*
> *Stirring the cauldron of doubt,*
> *As the dynamic dynamo refuses flight*
> *In a world that is more dark than light.*

Without warning, Adam rushed into the room, as the door was unlocked. Seeing Lynton standing there naked was such a shock he mumbled, "I, I, I, the door. It was unlocked. Oh my, I, I, I."

Lynton moving to the bed, picking up her gown and slipping it on, said with a smile, "It is O.K., I am sure that I am not the first woman you have ever seen naked, and I hope I will not be the last. Put that drooping tongue back in your mouth and tell me what is so important that you burst into a woman's boudoir unannounced."

Hanging his head with embarrassment, he muttered, "I am sorry, so sorry, but there has been another murder, and they were chasing the culprit outside the hotel. Didn't catch him, though."

The image of Lynton naked was so burned into Adam's brain that he could not get his mind off the glory of her body. She had her gown on now, but he knew what was under that silky covering that dangled around a body so daringly gorgeous that it would make a Catholic bishop kick in a stained glass window. He stepped back, trying not to look longingly at her, as if she were the sun, yet he saw her, like the sun, burning with sensual intensity, even as he bowed his head to try and control his raging hormones. To him, she seemed so beautiful, so seductive, so different from any other woman he had ever known. He was humbled before her grandeur. She was beautiful, but beautiful in the way a forest fire was beautiful, something to be admired from a distance, not up close, because if you got too close you might get burned and Adam was burning now; he was aflame, blazing with passion for the dynamic dynamo.

Lynton, used to men drooling over her, said, "Calm yourself and tell me the details."

Adam made his way to the sofa, as Lynton placed her blouse, which was on the bed, discretely over the letter-opener, as she did not want to have to explain what she, herself, did not understand.

Poor Adam was trying to control his thoughts, but that image of Lynton naked was like a brand burned deep into his brain. As she moved toward him, he lost the ability to speak, while he stared at her smooth graceful movements toward the chair on his immediate left. Her eyes were deeply dark, as dark as raw chocolate, dark as the blackest coffee, dark as the night. They were set in a fair face, oval with puffy little cherub-like cheeks. Her demeanour was like a soft, delicate teardrop on a tender cheek. Her easy smile could stop any man's heart, or maybe make it race so fast a heart attack was imminent. Her lips were thick, succulent, luscious and always had that freshly licked look as if minutes before you saw her she had been eating strawberries, and they made you want to taste their sweetness. No matter where she stood, she was in the centre of the room and all eyes were glued upon her. Yet, she was not loud, garish, ostentatious or vain. She got stares, because she was like a fire that flickers, glowing with a radiance that warmed and delighted all in her presence. There was a lambent light about her that glowed with a soft radiance, but what drew men to her fire was the warmth felt from the soul of a grand and glorious woman with great depth of character. However, she was more than a warm fire; she could be a raging inferno of desire.

Realizing that Adam was mesmerized with thoughts of carnal delights, Lynton made sure not to cross her legs. She snapped her fingers and said, "Earth to Adam. Come in Adam."

Adam snapped out of his trance and said, "I am always apologizing for my rude behaviour. I am so sorry."

LYNTON AND THE STELLENBOSCH TERROR

"It isn't rude behaviour Adam. It is complimentary behaviour, but there is a time and place for everything. I need to know about what happened."

Still, the effect she had on Adam was not so easily controlled. If you went out in the early days of winter in Canada, after the first cold snap of the season, one might understand what was happening to Adam. If you found a pool of water with a sheet of ice across the top, fresh and clear as glass, near the shore, the ice will hold you. However, if you go out farther and farther, eventually you will find the place where the surface just barely supports your weight. There you will feel what Adam felt. The ice splinters under your feet. Look down and you can see the white cracks darting through the ice like intricate, elaborate spider-webs. It is perfectly silent, but you can feel the sudden sharp vibrations through the bottoms of your feet. That is what happened when Adam got around Lynton. He was trying his heart out, but it just wasn't working very well, and Lynton knew it, but what could she do? She was who she was, and she could not change that. It absolutely did not matter whether she was naked or fully clothed. The effect was always the same.

She eased back in her chair and almost pleaded with Adam. "Please. Can you tell me about what has happened?"

"It is the murder this time of a visitor from a nearby village, but a well-known man named Adolph Mennamon."

Recalling Adam's penchant for tales, she smiled as she said, "I may regret this, but tell me all about it, please."

Almost giggling, Adam replied. "Well, all the details may take awhile, but Adolph Mennamon is, I mean was, an interesting person."

"He actually lives on a vast estate in Kleingoluk, but it has been a failing winery for years, and he has just managed to hold on. His father was a retired civil servant who tried his hand at growing grapes and producing what he hoped would be some fine wine. Well, it was a bit mediocre, but they have managed to hold on all these years. He, the father, that is, died many years ago. The road to his place is very old and narrow and when you get to the area where the estate is the forest opens in an irregular and very picturesque glade before its gate, and at the right a steep Gothic bridge carries the road over a stream that winds in deep shadow through the woods. It gives the impression of being a very lonely place. Now, you are going to ask what this has to do with his death today, and I am not sure, but I think it imperative that you know on that bridge over the stream, several months back, he saw exactly what Harold saw that night so many years ago when he was going home, across the same bridge. Yes, it was the same black cloaked figure with sorrowful red eyes. A few months ago, after seeing this figure, like Harold, Adolph lost his wife and child to a sudden illness that no one could explain. There, on a hilltop is a ruined village, with an abandoned roofless church where the graveyard is filled with moulding tombs of the proud family of Krupp, now all gone, who once owned the entire area. Respecting the cause of the desertion of this striking and melancholy spot, there is a legend which I shall relate to you another time, as I know you want the immediate facts as they relate to what happened last night. You see, I knew Adolph well, and he related to me some strange occurrences after his wife and child died. The first occurrence, as he told me awhile back, was in an old nursery, where his daughter, who died at 12, had spent her younger days. He was in it, reminiscing, and he was vexed at finding himself feeling a presence in the room. He saw a solemn, but very pretty face looking at him from the side of the bed. It was that of a middle-aged but beautiful lady who was kneeling, with her hands under the covers. At first, he thought it not a ghost, but just a trick of his mind, so he walked over to it, and to his surprise, she reached up and gently stroked his arm. He felt immediately delightfully soothed and almost hypnotized. He crawled onto the bed and fell asleep. He was awakened by a sensation, as if a sharp object was being placed into his breast very deep, and he shouted. The lady who had touched him previously, with a sharp object in her hand, started backward, with her eyes fixed on him, and then slipped down upon the floor, and, suddenly a giant bat was in the room, flittering about until it flew out the open window."

"He looked under the bed and all about the room, but there was no woman. He felt his chest and there was a slight indentation in his shirt, right over his heart. He asked himself if his dream was so real he had actually caused the indentation."

"Now, remember this tale is exactly as it was told to me by Adolph. After this occurrence, he realized that he had seen the woman before, but he could not remember where. It took a few days, but her image became clearer and clearer over time. It was someone he had seen going up to the Krupp estate, someone who had passed him in a chauffeured car as he went by her in the opposite direction. He kept going into the room constantly in hopes she would appear again. As far as I know she did not. He called me last night around midnight and said he was coming to see me with some news, news that would make my toes curl. He never made it. All I know is what occurred according to what I heard from the constable who said Adolph's body was found near here, and that there was someone leaning over him in a dark cloak and that a few people came upon the scene and chased the cloaked figure as they frantically shouted, 'the terror, the terror.' The figured seemed to float more than run. That is all I know at this point."

Lynton sighed and said, "So, we shall obviously never know what he wanted to tell you. What it was that could not wait until the morning."

"No, it seems that whatever was in this room is now free, free to roam about the whole Stellenbosch area, free to initiate a reign of terror."

Chapter 5

Blood on the Blade

A shadow in the darkness,

A phantom in the night,

You can feel it's presence,

You fear it might come into sight.

A ghost, a ghoul, a goblin, a disgusting fiend,

Shrouded in shadow, identity not gleaned,

A dark, foreboding creature of the night.

Demon of the darkness, it feeds upon your fright,

Hiding in the dark shadows,

Its nature yet unclear.

LYNTON AND THE STELLENBOSCH TERROR

The evil of this phantom legend's song
Spawns nightmares you should fear.
You shiver and quiver, praying for dawn!

It was a dire evening, and through it all there was Lynton, a vision of lace and flesh that seemed to glide into the heart of Adam. It was dawn now, and the gathering light collected around her body like it was coming home to wrap itself in contentment.

She was like a Shakespearean sonnet waiting to unfold from a parchment of parsimonious pleasures. Upon the morning breeze that was filtering through the open window her coal-black hair was flittering as she moved her head from side to side. The sweet light beyond all radiance burning in her dark eyes danced in harmonious rhapsody. In her face there seemed to come an air of purity, true beyond compare. Life's glory was burning tenderly upon her rhythmically heaving breasts. The grandeur and raw gloriousness of womanhood made her seem not like a mortal. She rose now from the chair as though she bore an angel's form, and her pursing lips foretold of coming words with a sound that simple human voices lacked. They were of a heavenly spirit, a living sun was about to pour forth with the warmth of a goddess of light.

Adam was anticipatory, sitting quietly, following Lynton with his eyes as she glided like a gazelle to the window, looked out at the street and said, "There is great mischief afoot here. I have been in the bowls of the earth, enduring the raging fires of the Taal volcanic inferno in the Philippines. I have battled the mighty Belmoda in the lair of the damned. I have matched wits with entities in haunted houses. I have chased supposed Aswangs into their dens of evil. I have been in the Karoo and stood against vampires with insatiable appetites for blood. Yet, this place, where we stand now, seems to carry an unparalleled evil, an evil that appears to defy all explanations. There is an evil here that seems to be dancing a waltz of death inside these four walls, but so malevolent is this thing, so determined to spread its vileness that it cannot be contained herein. It seeks freedom of movement to spread its evil."

"What are we to do, Lynton? How can we combat this terror?"

Lynton, smiling broadly replied, "We start by you leaving, so I can get dressed and then by eating an early breakfast."

They shared a laugh together and it appeared that she had broken Adam's amorous intensity for a little while at least. When Adam left, she walked over to the bed, removed the blouse that was covering the letter opener, picked up the object of her concern and held it up before her glistening eyes. How did it get out of that drawer and why?

At breakfast, they met a constable who was asking if anyone had noticed anything usual on the night of Mennamon's death. Of course, Lynton never mentioned the mystery of the letter opener. She did ask what happened to the man who was chased, and shaking his head vigorously, the constable replied, "That is the strangest thing of all. You see, they chased the willowy figure in a black cloak into an alley, a dead-end, if you will, and he just disappeared into thin air."

"Disappeared?" interjected Adam."

"Yes, into thin air. Some said he seemed to float upward, almost as if flying, the cloak acting as some type of wings."

Lynton said, "And, of course, the victim, Mr. Mennamon, his heart had been pierced twice with a very small, sharp instrument. Am I correct?"

"Yes, that is correct, and why would you know that? It is a detail that has not been released."

Adam then explained to the constable why Lynton was there, and the stern and proper lawman shrugged his shoulders and said, "All poppycock this stuff about an entity here in the hotel, and on that old Kleingeluk bridge. Poppycock I tell you, nothing but old tales people embrace in ignorance."

Lynton was taking it all in with great interest, and forming in her mind was a road map of happenstance going all the way back to that night that Harold had encountered the figure on the bridge. She was trying to connect the dots, but they were too obscure at this point.

Adam suddenly looked over at his mother and said, "Oh my, Leonard Lambert is due today. I must prepare his suite."

A dark gloom ascended upon the constable as he said, "Oh my, I am sorry Adam, but there was another death last night outside town, a Mr. Lambert, probably on his way here. He was found slumped over his steering wheel. Apparently the poor man had a heart attack."

Lynton sighed as she said, "I suggest you look for two small, barely perceptible wounds around his heart. You will find his heart was stopped by a small piercing object. He was murdered, just as Mr. Mennamon was. Perhaps you should come to my room; there is an instrument there that may be the murder weapon for both these deaths, and also Mr. Drummond's."

Entering her room, Lynton could sense the suspicions about her role in this whole affair were beginning to form in the constable's mind. She thought to herself that her dear Wayne was going to be really upset with her for getting involved.

Lynton led the constable to the table and pointed at the drawer. "It is in there."

He slowly pulled out the drawer. It was empty. Adam and Lynton stared at one another in puzzlement.

The constable said, "And just where is it my dear Ms. Viñas?"

"It was there. I have no idea what could have happened to it."

Adam said, "Constable Reed, I can attest to the fact that it was there. It has been in this room, as it was the one that killed my grandmother."

Cecile walked in just as Adam was explaining the predicament and said, "Yes, it has been there, but how it got here from the police evidence room, we do not know. I can verify it is the same one. I even used it as a child."

Looking over at Lynton, Constable Reed said, "Well, obviously it is not here now. And Ms. Viñas I think it would be very wise of you not to leave Stellenbosch for the time being. Do you understand?"

"Of course," replied Lynton.

The constable left and Adam apologetically said to Lynton, "I am so sorry that I got you into this mess."

Smiling, Lynton replied, "Well, I am in more trouble with Wayne than the police. He keeps telling me to stay out of trouble, but it just seems to always find me."

It was then that the desk clerk walked in with a letter, and handing it to Adam, said, "From Mr. Rhinehart, delivered by his secretary a few moments ago. She said he was too distraught to speak to you in person."

Cecile walked out with the clerk while Lynton and Adam sat on the sofa. There was a deep melancholia pervading that infernal room now, a sense that intense misery and sadness was descending upon Stellenbosch.

The letter was so extraordinary, so vehement, and in some places so self-contradictory, that one could only assume that it must have been written under the heavy burden of a man losing his most beloved possession.

It said, *"I have lost my darling daughter, whom I loved so much. I had no idea of her danger. I have lost her, and now it is too late. There is a fiend lose, a terror in Stellenbosch. What a fool have I been! I devote my remaining days to tracking and extinguishing a monster. At present, there is scarcely a gleam of light to guide me. I curse my conceited incredulity. Soon I shall devote myself for a time to enquiry, which may possibly lead me in pursuit of this evil thing. Sometime, if I still live, I will see you and I will then tell you all that I scarce dare put upon paper now. Farewell my friend, for I am about to pursue that which may kill me. I dare not tell the police, because they will think I am mad."*

The day had turned into night now and it was a soft clear evening, and the two loitered, speculating upon the possible meanings of the somewhat incoherent letter. They decided on journey to Kleingeluk to meet personally with Eric Rhinehart. The road was dark and foreboding, but fortunately the moon was shining brilliantly. As they neared the bridge where the original apparition was seen, on their left the narrow road wound away under clumps of shrub trees, and was lost to sight amid the thickening forest. At the right, the same road crossed the steep and picturesque bridge, near which stood a ruined tower that once guarded the pass; and beyond the bridge an abrupt hill rose, covered with trees, and showing in the shadows some grey ivy-clustered rocks.

Over the area and lower grounds, a thin film of mist was stealing like smoke, marking the distances with a transparent veil; and here and there the two travellers could see the Eerste River faintly flashing in the moonlight. It was a soft and serene scene, but there was loneliness to it, almost like the loneliness of the grave. The effect of the full moon in such a state of brilliancy was manifold. It acted on dreams, it acted on lunacy, it acted on nervous people, it had marvellous physical influences connected with life, but it also shone on death.

As they approached the entrance to the single lane bridge, a large black sedan came roaring across from the opposite side, approaching them like a raging hurricane pounding ashore. The excitement of the scene was made more painful by the clear, long-drawn screams of a female voice from inside the car. Adam slammed on his brakes before getting onto the bridge.

Lynton knew what was coming. She covered her eyes and turned her head away. Curiosity opened her eyes, and she saw a scene of utter confusion. The car had missed the turn after it crossed the bridge and had tumbled onto its side. Two men were busy climbing from the car, and pulled a beautiful lady with a commanding air out, who stood with clasped hands. Another very young woman was lifted from the car, appearing to be lifeless. Lynton and Adam were by now beside the older lady, tendering what aid they could. The older lady did not appear to notice anything, or to have eyes for anything but the slender girl who was being placed against the slope of the bank.

Lynton approached the young lady and surmised she was not dead, only stunned. Lynton reached down and took her cold, clammy hand. The lady clasped her hand and looked upward, as if in the momentary state of gratitude; but immediately she sat up with a death-like blank stare.

Lynton was taken with the younger lady's subdued but natural beauty that still shone through the current turmoil. Both women were dressed in black velvet, and looked rather pale, almost corpse-like, but with a proud and commanding countenance, though now agitated.

The older woman said, "Woe is me to have such a calamitous life. Here I am on a journey of life and death, in prosecuting which to lose an hour is possibly to lose all. My child will not have recovered sufficiently to resume her route for who can say how long. I must leave her. I cannot, dare not, delay. How far on, sir," she said to Adam, "can you tell, is Stellenbosch? I must leave her there; and shall not see my darling, or even hear of her until my return. I have a meeting to make, and I shall be gone a week at least."

Lynton interrupted. "Do not fear, if you will entrust her to our care, we are at the Stellenbosch Inn. We shall see to her safety."

Adam was surprised, but not shocked. He nodded his head in agreement with Lynton.

The woman said, "My daughter has just been disappointed by a cruel misfortune, in a visit from which she had long anticipated a great deal of happiness."

"If you confide this young lady to our care it will be her best consolation. If, as you say, you cannot suspend your journey and you must part with her this very night there is absolutely nowhere you do so with more honest assurances of care and tenderness than here with us. I am Adam Kruger of Stellenbosch and this is Lynton Viñas."

"My, oh my," said the lady. "I know of you Ms. Viñas, and how fortuitous to meet the renowned demon hunter. I wish I had known you were here earlier."

There was something in this lady's air and appearance so distinguished, even imposing, and in her manner so engaging, as to impress one, quite apart from the dignity she displayed, with a conviction that she was a person of consequence.

By this time, the car was back upright as a result of the two burly men pushing it over. The lady threw on her daughter a glance which was less affectionate than one might have anticipated; then she beckoned slightly to Adam, and withdrew two or three steps with him out of hearing; and talked to him with a fixed and stern countenance. Less than a minute at most she remained thus employed, then she turned, and a few steps brought her to where her daughter lay. She kneeled beside her for a moment and whispered, then hastily kissed her and stepped into the car that was now purring with a racing engine ready to dash away. The door was closed, and the car sped off at a furious pace, making one wonder if they might well crash again. And why had it turned around and headed back the way from which it came? It went up the hillside toward a mansion.

Lynton and Adam stood dumbfounded that a woman would leave her injured daughter. They watched spellbound, as the car's taillights gradually faded into the distance up the hillside.

Nothing remained to assure them that the adventure had not been an illusion until the young lady turned her head, evidently looking about her, and in a very sweet voice asked complainingly, "How fortuitous to have found two such nice people to stay with while my mother fulfills an urgent mission."

Dispensing with their journey to see Eric Rhinehart, Adam and Lynton drove the young woman, who introduced herself as Susan Louder, and her mother as the Countess Karin Louder of Romania, back to the hotel, where she was settled into room 228 across the hall from Lynton. A doctor was called, but she steadfastly refused to be examined. As she settled comfortably in bed,

Lynton, her curiosity aroused, pulled up a chair beside her.

They were talking over the adventure of the evening when Susan asked, "And what of Linda. She never got out of the over turned car did she?"

Lynton said, "Someone else was in the car?"

"Yes, Linda."

Susan closed her eyes and drifted off to sleep as Adam, standing at the edge of the bed with a grim look on his face, said, "There is no particular reason why I should not tell you, but the countess expressed a reluctance to trouble us with the care of her daughter, saying she was in delicate health, and nervous. She was about to make a journey of vital importance, and why she did not want to share it with you I do not know. However, she emphasized it needed to be very rapid and secret. She further said, 'Susan will be silent about what I am up to, so do not try to ply it from her.' That is all she said. When she said the word secret, she paused for a few seconds. I fancy she makes a great point of that. You saw how quickly she was gone. I hope I have not done a very foolish thing, in taking charge of this young lady."

The next morning, Susan was sitting up; her slender figure enveloped in a soft silk dressing gown taken from the bag that had been left behind by her mother. It was embroidered with flowers, and lined with thick quilted silk, but it was still depressingly black in colour.

Cecile, for the first time, got a good look at the young girl, and paleness descended over her. She turned as white as a ghost. She motioned for Lynton and Adam to come into the hallway.

"I have seen that girl before, I know it" said Cecile.

"Where?" asked Adam.

"With my grandmother, in room 227, so many years ago. I walked into her room once and sitting there on the sofa beside her was, I know it sounds impossible, but it was this woman. I will never forget it, because my grandmother acted as if there was no one there beside her. When I told her that I wanted to meet the pretty lady, all she said was in a curt way 'what lady?' I was flabbergasted. I left, but I tell you this girl was she. I can never forget that face, that death-like expression."

Suddenly, the three noticed in the doorway, Susan, staring with a surprised countenance as she said, "And I recognize you. I have seen you before; in a dream I had night after night, a young girl the spitting image of you, only younger, staring me in the face as I sat silently on a sofa."

Susan's countenance had softened, and Lynton said, "You need your rest. You have undergone a frightening ordeal."

Lynton guided her back to bed and sat beside her as Adam and Cecile stood at the foot of the bed. Looking directly at Adam, Susan said, "I also have had a dream, several dreams about you. I must tell you my vision about you; it is so very strange. I awoke from a confused and troubled dream, and found myself in a room, a very dark room. The bed in the room was empty, and the room itself without anyone but myself in it; and I, after looking about for some time, heard someone crying; and looking behind me, I saw you. You look as you do now. I moved toward you and you put your arms around me, and comforted me. I was suddenly aroused by a dark figure behind you and slipped down from your arms, and, it seemed to me, lost consciousness for a moment; then I awakened back in my room, but your face I have never forgotten. It was so kind, so serene and peaceful."

It was then that Adam said, "I have never told of this before, but I too have had vivid dreams. If you were less pretty I think I should be very much afraid of you, but being as you are, and being so young, I feel only that I have made your acquaintance years ago, and have already a right to your intimacy; it does seem as if we were destined to be friends. I wonder whether you feel as strangely drawn towards me as I do to you; I have never had a friend, a real friend and I dreamed of this beautiful young lady often, and she looked exactly as you do now. She would look after me."

LYNTON AND THE STELLENBOSCH TERROR

Lynton observantly took all this in with her keen intellect. Were they drawn instinctively to each other, or was there something more sinister about their dreams?

The next day saw Adam and Susan being inseparable. She was slender, and wonderfully graceful in all her actions. Except that her movements were languid. Her complexion was pale and sullen; her features were small and beautifully formed; her eyes large, dark and shiny; her hair was quite lustrous, thick and long when it was down about her shoulders. Still, Lynton and Adam, despite his growing amorous interest in Susan, both discerned something dark beneath her surface. Susan exercised with respect to herself, her mother, her history, everything in fact connected with her life, plans, and people, an ever resolute reserve in the dissemination of information.

While all this was occurring, Lynton had looked endlessly for that accursed dagger-like letter opener to no avail. The room had been filled with quiet and there were no sinister manifestations. Yet, there was always that feeling in the quarters, a feeling that you simply were not alone.

At the close of day, the sun sliding slowly behind the mountains in the distance, Lynton lay down on the bed, sighed and simply stared at the ceiling in contemplation of all that had happened. She was not asleep, but was in that twilight world where all semblance of being awake was slowly fading. Suddenly, and without fear she saw a dark, cloaked figure hovering overhead. She could not arise. It was as if some unseen force was applying pressure to her body, not allowing her to get up and flee the accursed room. Still, she was not afraid. Yet, she began to breathe heavily in a strained rhythmic pattern that allowed her to listen intently to her beating heart.

She looked over at the table where her cell phone was charging. She felt the urge to reach for it and text Wayne about her predicament and say she was leaving and freeing herself from this horrible ordeal, but she could not move.

The figure over her hovered menacingly and she continued to struggle to get up, but she was totally paralyzed. Then those sorrowful eyes bore into her psyche, but there was no fear in her, and the figure suddenly appeared less menacing.

If she had been a religious person, she would have prayed, but, for her, that was not an option. She tried to close her eyes to blot out that threatening cloaked figure above the bed, but it was impossible to shut them. She could not even blink.

The intense darkness pervaded all about until the morning sunlight began to filter under the drawn drapes, then the cloaked figure slowly dissipated as her ability to move returned. She tilted her head toward the nightstand where her phone was charging and there it was - the damned knife-like letter opener. How long had it been there? Who or what had placed it in the table? Oh my, there was blood on the blade.

Chapter 6

Last Hope in Ending This Terror

There is something dark in the river by Babylon.

Dear Leonard Cohen I somewhat borrow here.

By the rivers dark she wandered on.

She living her life there in Babylon.

And she did not forget her holy song.

When she had no strength in Babylon.

Was she singing in those days of a girl on the go?

Of someone called Lynton, the dynamic dynamo?

By the rivers dark, where she could not see

LYNTON AND THE STELLENBOSCH TERROR

Who was waiting there? Who was hunting her?
And she cut her lip. And she searched his heart,
As she sipped from the river dark.
A dark spectre hovered over her,
And she saw there its wondering heart.
Could she keep herself from evil apart?

She could not know and she could not see
Who was waiting there; who was hunting her.
By the rivers dark she proceeded on.
She belonged at last to Babylon.
Then the spectre struck her heart
With a deadly force, and it said,
"This heart - it is not yours."

And she fought the spectre's whirling wind,
Never bowing before the smoky ring.
The spectre circled her with everything,
By the rivers dark, in a wounded dawn.
She, if necessary would give her life in Babylon.
Even, if never again to sing the scared song,
She came to defeat the evil all along?

J. WAYNE FRYE

LYNTON AND THE STELLENBOSCH TERROR

From a withered limb, both song and tree,
They sang for her: "Be the truth unsaid."
Blessing is never gone, never forgetting Babylon.
She did not know, and she could not see
Who was waiting there? Who was hunting her?
By the rivers dark, where it all goes on;
By the rivers dark in Babylon.

She was now before the river so dark,
And she had tasted of its evil heart.
Who or what was waiting there for her?
Had it all along been hunting for her?
Was it Lynton's fate to be lured here?
By the rivers dark, where it all goes on,
By the rivers dark in Babylon?

Examining the letter opener, Lynton knew that since she was under suspicion, it would be best not to inform anyone of its reappearance. She went into the bathroom, wiped the blood off and placed it back into the drawer. She showered and dressed, anxious to read the morning paper, because she instinctively knew that someone had died during the night, no doubt, with a pierced heart indicating an insertion of the knife-like letter opener.

Sure enough, there had been another questionable death. A homeless man was found in the back alley with fear burned into his face and two puncture wounds to his heart drained of blood. That was the topic of discussion over breakfast, and afterward, Adam, as they went upstairs, said to Lynton, "I have asked the impossible of you. Things were never this bad before. That monstrous thing was corralled in that room, but by bringing you here, I have unleashed hell. It has been stirred by your presence. I feel responsible for all these deaths somehow."

"You are responsible for nothing Adam. I am sorry too that this seems to have been precipitated by our meddling, but there is something else we do not yet understand at play here, something that, if you will stick with me and see this through, will finally bring an end to the curse that hangs over this place like a dark cloud ready to burst forth with a furious storm raining down destruction. Do not give up. There is a pattern to all this, a pattern I cannot yet understand or explain just yet, but I do not give up."

"I am determined then, Lynton, determined to stand by your side."

Later in the day, Cecile brought down into room 227, where Susan was chatting with Lynton and Adam, some old boxes from the attic. She laughed, saying, "At my age I love to reminisce. I thought all of you might enjoy helping me go through these old photographs and objects from way back when my great grandmother lived here, I have not seen this stuff since I was a child."

Always fascinated by history, Lynton was eager, but Adam and Susan exhibited a lacklustre interest, almost as if it was something they would endure out of courtesy. Susan sat looking listlessly on, while one after the other, the old pictures, nearly all of people, were brought to the light of day for the first time in many years. The dust of time had all but obliterated many of them, and there were a few hand painted small portraits from a time before photography was refined. Lynton was particularly interested in those and asked questions about them, which were unanswerable.

Suddenly, Cecile removed one item that was wrapped in a dusty white linen cloth. It was a small hand painted picture, about a foot high, and nearly square, in a simple frame; but it was so blackened by age that it was not discernable. There was a date carved into the frame – 1919. Cecile took the linen cloth and started rubbing off the thick dust, causing her to sneeze. Then, all there were startled. The person in the picture was easily recognizable. It was the spitting image of Susan.

Adam blurted out, "Susan, my, oh my, it is you. I cannot believe it. It simply is not possible, but there you are."

He took the picture; examined it closely as Susan sat there showing no emotion. He stretched out his hands and held it under the light, looking at the tiny mole on the right side of the woman's right collar bone, which was exposed.

LYNTON AND THE STELLENBOSCH TERROR

Lynton, noticing it, looked down at Susan and said, "Your blouse is high upon your neck Susan. Would you show us your collar bone, please?"

Without a word, she very slowly and deliberately lowered the blouse neckline. There was the same mole in the same place.

Susan said, "Certainly it is a wonderful likeness," but she looked away, and to Lynton's surprise seemed unfazed.

"Coincidence," said Adam.

"Perhaps," replied Lynton.

Lynton took the portrait and turned it over, and on the back it read, "The Countess Karin Louder."

Susan, leaning back in her seat, her fine eyes under their long lashes gazing on Lynton in contemplation, smiled in a kind of rapture. "Perhaps that explains the likeness. My mother's great grandmother was, like her, named Karin. But why and how did that photo get here?"

Lynton asked, "And the night of your accident your mother was leaving, but you and she were fleeing in haste from where?"

"From the home of Eric Rhinehart. That is all I can tell you. We were there on a quest, a quest for some answers."

Lynton, wishing she and Adam had finished their journey to Eric Rhinehart's, said, "You cannot share the purpose of your journey there?"

"Only with my mother's permission, I cannot betray her wish that I tell no one of why we were there."

Not wanting to press the matter, Lynton said, "Good enough. We shall not pressure you at this time, but Adam received a frantic note from Eric Rhinehart about something happening to his daughter. His exact words were, "I have lost her." Can you explain that?"

Susan looked perplexed as she said, "I cannot at this time."

"Do you think," asked Lynton with seriousness, "that she is dead?"

"I can't say."

Lynton, her inquiring mind now racing rapidly, said, "Tell me this, if you will. I noticed there was an old castle on the hillside, deserted I believe, and I saw a car's headlights coming down that hillside before your car appeared at the bridge. You did not come directly from Rhinehart's place. You stop by that castle first."

"We did, yes. You see my mother's family was ruined financially long ago, leaving her only with a title and that castle was once owned by her family. Then, it was bought by the Krupp family, but it fell into receivership and has sat empty for many years. She just wanted to see it; see it and reminisce about what once was. We just drove by it and sped away."

"How interesting," Lynton said, languidly.

The hour was very late, and they left for bed. Lynton interestingly noticed Adam took the portrait with him.

Adam's mother went downstairs, and Lynton stood by the door, watching Adam and Susan walk into room 228 together. She smiled and giggled slightly, thinking of Wayne. Romance was about to come into full fruition between those two.

As Lynton stood in the doorway of room 227, she looked back at room 228 and saw the lights inside the room filter out under the door into the hallway, and in an instance they were switched off. She smiled again, and thought of how glorious romance was, and she was glad Adam, being such a nice fellow, had apparently found himself someone who was going to willingly respond to his romantic overtures, but Lynton wondered about Susan and what she was hiding.

The next morning at breakfast, Lynton was sitting by herself when a giggling pair of new lovers came into the restaurant. They took a seat at Lynton's table and ordered breakfast, and very sheepishly stared at Lynton, who said, "My, you two certainly look very chipper this morning. You must have both had a good night's sleep," and then she giggled a bit, as she continued, "or if not a good night's sleep, at least a good night."

Adam and Susan looked at one another and smiled, then looked at Lynton. Adam said, "You are a tease, Lynton Viñas."

"No, I am just someone who really enjoys romance."

They shared a laugh and Lynton said to Susan, "Has your mother not texted you since she left?"

She answered, "No."

Lynton said, "Text her then."

Ignoring the request from Lynton which would have elicited a response perhaps detailing her mother's location, Susan bowed her head. Lynton, probing now, said, "And where would you be going Susan if you joined her?"

Again, ignoring the question, Susan said, "I have caused all of you here enough trouble. I dare not tell you where she is for your own good."

"Tell us or not," interjected Adam. "It does not matter, and you are no burden to us. Please stay until your mother returns."

Lynton got up, looked back at Adam and Susan, and reflected on what Wayne had written in one of his books. "Her flesh is like freshly woven fine silk. When I glide my hand gently over her dark brown body it flows with the smoothness of hot butter spread on warm bread. What comfort there is in the skin of someone you love." Oh, how she missed her husband, who always had praise for her and a word to boost her when she was low. She reflected on what he had once told her as they lay together in rapturous harmony. "I love feeling your warmth, a radiating heat that pulsates in proclamation of your womanliness. I glide my hand gently over a perfectly formed body, down over your taunt stomach and linger there, kneading your softness. This is not sex. This is the discourse of adoration." She wondered about Susan, because there was a physical coldness to her, as when Lynton had inadvertently touched her, she was physically cold. Was she mentally cold as well?

She walked into room 227 with tears streaming down her cheeks. She missed Wayne so much, and seeing Susan and Adam together made her long for the sound of his voice.

She got on line and poured her heart out to Wayne on Skype, detailing all that had happened. He adored her so much, but he could not help chiding her for once again getting involved in an adventure that might be dangerous. She was supposed to have left that life behind, but he knew better than to tell her to let it go. As he would often say to her, "Sometimes your will is like a brick wall, and I would be just as successful talking to brick wall as telling you to not go forward when confronted with a mystery."

Lynton is a woman who speaks with her heart. There is a glowing energy within her petite brown frame that tears through the cosmos like a comet soaring endlessly into the oblivion of space lighting up the darkness. This woman is a Shakespearean sonnet of stardust sprinkled into the world. This is nature's finest pronouncement of perfection. For men and even women, she lights fire to souls and diminishes resistance. She makes people realize that fire can heal scars of misery as she burns with intensity. And her intensity over a series of deaths and the mysterious nature of Susan, as well as the comments by Eric Rhinehart in his message to Adam were now roaring through her mind like a raging river through a gorge. She sensed there was something she had missed, something that was a key to what was going on. Why hadn't she stayed in Cape Town? No, she had to relax by taking a train to Stellenbosch. Relax! Yeah, she was really relaxing!

Lynton was always a sceptic, so she knew that sometimes dreams can be so real that spectres seem never to wear out or to die, but renew their tissue both of person and of raiment in marvellous fashion, so that certain events make them more relentlessly and recklessly persistent. Had her coming to Stellenbosch actually stirred this spirit? Was she the catalyst that initiated this reign of terror? Was she a conduit that opened a portal that pulsated with evil intent? Was she the indirect cause of all these deaths? Or, was she the actual somnambulist culprit with the bloody letter opener in that infernal room?

In a world where poverty abounds, a large percentage of people embrace fairy tales as their only real hope for a better life. Thus, ghosts are born with men in all ages and in all lands, as for many, they offer proof of that ever fervent belief in an after–life. If there are malevolent forces practicing evil from beyond the grave, then why would there not be angels, guardian angels to offer protection and be guides to eternity?

It is difficult to establish the apostolic succession of spooks in actual life, but in literature, the line reaches back as far as primeval picture writing. If man believes in ghosts, or even better, sees them, are they not proof of an after-life?

The more man knows of natural laws, the keener he is about the supernatural. He may claim to have laid aside superstition, but time and again, superstitions work their way into acceptance by those who live lives of quit desperation. Although mankind has discarded witchcraft and alchemy, that other world, that realm of the undying dead fascinates him, piques his interest in what might lie beyond. Thus is the mind of Lynton Viñas, a born sceptic, but an astute observer of what seems impossible.

She sensed that if they were real that modern ghosts are less simple and primitive than their ancestors, and are developing complexes of various kinds. They are more democratic than of old, and have more of a diversity of interests, so that mortals have scarcely the ghost of a chance with them. They employ all the agencies and mechanisms known to mortals, and have, in addition, their own methods of transit and communication. Whereas, in the past, a ghost had to stalk or glide to its haunts, now it limousines, or helicopters, or airplanes or ubers, so that naturally the entity can get in more work than before. It travels all about in a variety of forms. Some of them even carry signs, proudly and boldly proclaiming the evil. How many times does one have to see an airplane like the one with the name Trump embossed on its side, a helicopter with a military emblem proclaiming "death from the air," a van with a corporate logo painted in bold letters with lies about how much it cares scrolled under it, a billboard with sexual innuendo to titillate people into buying what they don't need to realize that evil is about at all times in a variety of forms. A ghostly demon might actually offer much less deviltry than that perpetrated by the living, breathing and embodiment of evil prancing around in the form of corporations and the rich.

Still, it is the spectre that is feared most – the entity from beyond the grave. Ghosts vary in many respects. Some are like the pallid shades of the past, altogether unlike the living and with an unmistakable spectral form, or lack of it, as some ghosts cause more fear with grunts and groans that physical appearance. The dreadful presence of a ghost that one cannot see is more unbearable than the spectre that one can locate and attempt to escape from.

This spectre Lynton was confronting exhibited a physical form that swept like a mist through the air and fluttered about like dead leaves in a breeze. Its evil was not palpable, though. You could not taste its evil. It was scary, yes, but it was not an overpowering monstrosity of malevolence.

LYNTON AND THE STELLENBOSCH TERROR

The dynamic dynamo was tired of pussy-footing around. She had been polite and non-insistent, but now her patience was wearing thin. It was time to confront this evil head-on by refusing to politely defer to the sensibilities of people who were not sharing all they knew of this evil.

> *Menacing dark messenger,*
> *Robed like painted death,*
> *Whom do you seek*
> *In the darkness all about?*
> *My, oh my, is Lynton at risk?*
> *Will she by death be kissed?*

Lynton, ever the meek, polite girl with a passion for understanding could sometimes be so forceful that she bordered on being a storm trooper of indignation. Her tenacity and stubbornness were legendary. She burst into the hotel office where Cecile and Adam sat at a conference table sharing pleasantries with Susan. One who rarely used profanity, Lynton spoke with authority as she said, "You, Adam, asked me here to try and get to the bottom of a mystery, but I be damned if I can do that when people will not share the truth with me. I am asking all three of you if you want to see the murders terminated, if you want to see the horrible entity that has pranced with impunity about this inn and town stayed and stymied into irrelevance. Simply say yes or no."

The three sat in complete stunned silence for a few seconds before Cecile, after a deep breath, said, as she looked at the other two at the table, "Of course! I have lived with this horror all my life, and my son has endured it all his life. For us, I can say yes without equivocation. I cannot speak for Susan."

Susan contemplated for a long time in complete silence and with bowed head she slowly rose from the table, strolled toward the door slump shouldered, without uttering a single word. She unhurriedly turned the knob, gradually opened the door and walked out.

Adam started to get up, and as he did Lynton said, "Leave and so do I. I hate to ever give-up, but I refuse to work in the dark. I have helped others face the unknown, face evil and defeat it, but I am ready to end this charade and do as Susan did."

Cecile looked up at Adam and said, "Sit down my dear son. Sit and let us accede to the request of this dear woman who only wants to help us. She may be our only and absolute last hope to end this terror."

Chapter 7

Cold Chills Up and Down Your Spines

Oh entity that dances

with blackened heart,

so insanely jealous of the living,

when did your evil really start?

Breeding such desolate despair

you want to possess souls,

and sullenly lay them bare.

Feeding upon their

deepest darkest desires,

you ravish their hope

as your evil conspires,
dragging them down
to the pits of hell,
lost spirits enslaved,
captive under your spell.

Taking a seat at the conference table, Lynton said, "So, let us get one thing straight from the start. You Adam did not meet me by accident. You found out from what person that I would be travelling on the steam train here?"

"From a school employee named Andeswa, who is a friend of mine. She knew of our problems, and also knew of your reputation. She knew I was in Cape Town, and when you told her you would be travelling to Stellenbosch, she alerted me."

Smiling, Lynton said, "I'll deal with Andeswa when I get back to Cape Town. However, for now, you sir are in my crosshairs, so be very, very careful. As my husband can attest, I am not one with whom you want to trifle. And now, I know that your amorousness was also an act, which may make me even angrier."

Shaking his head vehemently, Adam, almost pleading said, "No, no, that was no act. I really do find you an alluringly attractive woman."

Letting out a light giggle, Lynton interjected with a jesting demeanour, "That my dear Adam is really playing with fire when you try to massage my ego. However, you did do a good job of it. I am no different than any other woman. We all like the attention of men, even those of us who are married."

Lynton continued with a more serious tone. "Your stories were all true I am certain, but you left out something important about Harold, perhaps you can tell me now what happened before he left here and proceeded home, or perhaps your mother would prefer to level with me, give me complete details on what happened that night."

Cecile, a look of admiration on her face, said, "You are a marvel my dear, an absolute marvel. Yes, there was something that happened before he encountered that demon on the bridge."

Lynton, with rock solid determination, interjected, "And just what occurred?"

Cecile looked at Adam and said, "You can tell it better than I. Go ahead."

Adam took a deep breath. "You are so right my dear Lynton when you say we knew about you. I went to Cape Town with hopes I would be able to see you there, but when I found out you were taking the train here, I decided a more subtle approach would be appropriate. I have read, naturally, of your battles with vampires and demons. What we have here in Stellenbosch is an evil that knows no bounds. It will remain dormant for long periods, then appear with suddenness, wreck havoc and then disappear for a time again. It is as if the evil fiend that haunts this place, feeds for awhile on death and then is satiated enough to quietly depart until it must feed on death again. And for some reason, it has made its home here. I cannot tell you how many times over the years we have thought that the evil was done with, only to have it reappear again and again, and the past two weeks it has been rampant, and we fear for our lives – my mother and I."

"And why do you think it is after you?"

He looked over at his mother, his eyes meeting hers with concern. He could not speak.

His mother offered a sombre assessment. "There was once a man in this hotel. He lived here, lived just down the hall from where you now reside. He was a quiet man, a professor who came here for relaxation. He was doing research on an ancient cult that used a ceremonial dagger to make sacrifices to the god Pan. He was interested in the people who were meeting at the Krupp estate, hiding from public scrutiny, always practicing their evil in darkness and the isolation of Kleingeluk. My grandmother was a participant. She was part of the ritual time and again over the years. The ritual involved tying down a person to be sacrificed and inserting a narrow, sharp-tipped dagger into the heart of the victim twice. It was actually a fairly painless death, and then someone sucked out the blood."

"Murder," interjected Lynton, "is still murder whether it is painless or not, and it was not someone sucking the blood but some thing."

Cecile, replied, "Yes, you are right, of course."

"The truth is your grandmother welcomed this evil then as a willing participant?"

"Yes."

Lynton was on a roll. "That letter opener is an ancient Egyptian ceremonial dagger. The group told her to kill the professor right?"

"Yes."

"They did not know you cannot kill a person who is already dead, which the professor was."

"What?" replied a shocked Adam and Cecile.

"I'll explain later. Right now, go on," offered Lynton.

"Well, the oddity is that as time went on, there were those in the cult who believed that there was a ritual they could follow that would give them immortality as long as they continued the sacrifices. The man who lived here, the professor, when my grandmother was still alive, found out that the cult was still functioning; still practicing the abominable ritual that they believed would give them immortality. He sat out to expose it."

Lynton interjected, "Was he a small built fellow, bald and slightly stooped shouldered?"

"He was, yes, but how…."

She interrupted her, "It is not important how I know that. The point is you assumed your grandmother murdered him?"

"You are amazing Lynton, just amazing. Yes, she did murder him to keep him quiet."

Lynton leaned forward, "As I said, you cannot murder someone who is already dead, but the point is that you assumed he was alive. And you saw the supposed murder. She committed it right here in the hotel, and she disposed of the body in room 227, by dividing the room and sealing the body up in the wall, and you did not know the reason she did that was because the cult to which she belonged believed a ghost could only be stayed by sealing it in a pine vault with silver tipped nails. The wall was the vault."

Shaking her head in disbelief, Cecile said, "Amazing! You are amazing."

Smiling, even letting out a little giggle, Lynton said, "That is what I keep telling my husband day in and day out. However, in regards to the professor, he had died long before you thought you saw your grandmother kill him. He had been a ghost since meeting with Harold that night before he left here to go home. Go on with what actually happened when the body was encased in the wall."

"I remember absolutely everything about it, down to the last detail. It was a concerted effort, and my mother was forced to help dispose of the body. I saw it all, as deep sea divers see what is going on above them, through a dense, rippling transparency. There was an evil about my grandmother I had never known. After that I became distant from her, and somewhat from my own mother."

Lynton felt sympathy for her having to live with this knowledge all those years. She turned to her with pity and said, "Unfortunately, far too many of us find out that our parents, or grandparents or many members of our families are not what they appear to be. I have experienced that myself."

She looked over at Adam, and offered some acceptance of his difficult predicament in getting her to the inn. "Don't fret about your subterfuge. I probably would not have come had you just confronted me with the truth, but, regardless, I am here now, and I am here until this evil is laid to rest, or it lays me to rest."

"Then you can see an explanation to this terror?"

"I can, yes, but at this point in my investigation I am not ready to completely reveal what I think is going on. You see, I have the germination of an idea, an idea that we have all been seeing this wrong from the very start. There is not just one entity here. There are two - two distinctly different entities."

"Oh my," offered Cecile.

Lynton had done her research, but she thought only a partial explanation was needed until she was surer of exactly what was going on. She could tell though that they needed more details. She continued. "There were two walls were they not?"

Cecile nodded her head affirmatively, and Lynton continued. "So, the outer wall had the silver tipped nails, but the inner wall did not. You remodelled, and replaced the outer wall with bead board, but were careful not to touch the inner wall, which you knew had a corpse behind it."

"Yes, you are right."

"So, after that bit of remodelling, there were more appearances of dark entities than before, because the containment had been altered. You were not aware of it of course, but there were always two entities, not one. Now, the one that was corralled had returned when the silver tipped nails were removed and its spirit freed."

She rose, and bid them adieu as they sat thinking over all that she had shared. The precautions of nervous people are infectious, and persons of a like temperament are pretty sure, after a time, to imitate them, but not Lynton, who went to her room with the intention of making it easy for that cloaked figure to find her waiting anxiously for its manifestation.

She looked into the drawer of the desk by the bed, and it was there – the letter opener dagger. She lay down and closed her eyes but not so tightly that she could not see. A light in the bathroom was still on, but she noticed the door slowly close and the room was bathed in darkness.

She ignored the closing door, assuming it was just an uneven hinging which made the door slowly creep shut from the uneven attachment. She was getting tired and drifted off into that twilight world between being awake and asleep, where dreams come through stone walls, light up dark rooms, or darken light ones, and where shadows make their exits and their entrances as they please.

She began what she thought was a dream. She was conscious of being in her room, and lying in bed, precisely as she actually was. She saw, or thought she saw, the room and its furniture just as it had been, except that it was very dark, and she saw something moving around the foot of the bed, which at first she could not accurately distinguish. But soon, it appeared as a lithe, sinister restless dark shadow. It was pacing. No, it was gliding back and forth at the foot of the bed like a beast in a cage. Its pace grew faster, and the room rapidly darker and darker, and at length so dark that she could no longer see anything of it but its fiery red eyes. She felt it spring lightly on the bed.

The two broad eyes approached her face, and suddenly she felt a stinging pain as if two large needles darted, a centremetre or two apart, slightly into her breast. She woke! Had she really been asleep? Had she imagined the image, imagined it jumping on the bed?

The darkness was all encompassing, but slowly she saw the figure forming again. It was more pronounced now as it took on shape, the shape of a man, but there was a hood on the black cloak and it now covered the head, and again, those red eyes were glowing like a raging fire in the darkness.

LYNTON AND THE STELLENBOSCH TERROR

There was not the slightest stir of sound except for Lynton's intense breathing, as she stared at the entity. The figure glided toward the door; then, stood by it, the door slowly opened, and it seemed to turn into a bat and flitter out.

What occurred was a transitory terror, for Lynton never succumbed to fear but for brief periods until she could gather her wits. She lay back in bed and looked to her right and instinctively pulled out the drawer of the desk. The letter opener dagger was gone, and there to her right was another dark figure, seeming to stand watch over her. It disappeared into the wall.

Lynton got up early the next morning, showered and quickly put on her clothes. She walked into the hallway and was greeted by Adam, who was on his way to breakfast. He had not come from Susan's room, so obviously they had not been engaged in a romantic interlude. They stood for a few seconds as they passed pleasantries, and down the hall came the kindly looking old bald man, who nodded at Lynton. She returned the greeting with her own responsive nod, while Adam just ignored him completely.

Susan came down late, just as Adam and Lynton were finishing up their breakfasts. She remarked, "I was so frightened last night. I heard strange noises in my room, as if something was stuck in the walls, some rat perhaps. I had a dream of something black coming around my bed, and I awoke in a perfect horror, and I really thought, for some seconds, I saw a dark figure near the window just looking out."

Cecile came in with the morning papers and Lynton said, "And there was no murder last night?"

"No."

"I am surprised, because the letter opener is gone."

"What?"

"I will not go into detail, only say that room 227 was a bit active last night, as apparently, so was Susan's room." Lynton turned to Susan and continued, "And you my dear girl, need to tell us, without equivocation, exactly where your mother went and why."

"I cannot; she swore me to secrecy."

"There is no need for secrecy, Susan, because I know why your mother was at the Krupp mansion and why she was in a hurry to flee with that woman who was in your car."

Susan abruptly got up, and stormed out without a word. All day and night there was no Susan around. In the morning, Adam knocked on her door. Lynton heard the knock, came out and said, "Get a pass key. This is not a good sign."

Hurriedly, Adam got the key. They opened the door and the room was empty except for her suitcase, and there was no indication she had been in the room at all. Lynton walked to the window at the end of the hall by the fire escape, which was open. She peered out and said, "She may have left by means of the fire escape."

They went back to her room. Inside the room, which was perfectly undisturbed, Lynton began to pace about. She examined everything there. It was past 8:00 A.M. They went down for breakfast, but when they came back around 9:00 A.M., Susan's door was wide open, and to the wonderment of Adam and Lynton, there, standing at her dressing table was Susan. They were astounded. Her face expressed surprise. "Last night has been a night of wonders," she said.

"Please explain," asked Lynton.

"It was just when darkness fell, when I went to sleep out of exhaustion and dismay. My door was locked. My sleep was uninterrupted, and, as far as I know, dreamless; but I woke just now on the sofa in the dressing room here. How could all this have happened without my being awakened? I have no idea where I have been. I simply woke up on the sofa with no recollection of how I got there," she said with what Lynton recognized as a lack of sincerity in her voice. She was lying.

Cecile joined them, taking a seat on the sofa beside Lynton while Susan and Adam sat on the edge of the bed side by side. Lynton said, "Forgive me, if I risk a conjecture and ask a question. Now, the marvel of last night consists in your having been removed from your bed and your room, without being awakened, and this removal having occurred apparently while the windows were still secured and the door locked from the inside. Did you have a dream, maybe?"

She contemplated for awhile and said, "My, I can remember seeing a dark figured. Yes, a dark figure, but not in here. It was in another room. Yes, in another room."

Lynton rose, took Susan by the hand and led her to room number 227. Look around and think, was this the room in your dream?"

"Yes, I think it was."

Lynton said, "I was gone last night for a brief time between 9 and 10. I went out for a stroll and walked to the Café Colman for some tea and a cinnamon bun. You came in then."

"But why, Lynton? Why would I come to your room?"

Lynton knew that Susan was not being completely honest. She walked over to the desk by the bed, pulled out the drawer and there it was, the letter opener, and on the tip was a blood stain. She turned to Adam and said, "Get the morning papers."

Adam returned holding up the paper, showing bold headlines on the front page: *Well Known Businessman Killed by Mysterious Method.*

Lynton said, as Adam began to read, "It was two small puncture wounds to his heart by a thin sharp object. However, I do not know who was killed. You can enlighten me on that."

Adam, a stunned look on his face, eased into a nearby chair, as he read who the victim was. He uttered in a slow, methodical, surprised tone, "Two puncture wounds to Eric Rhinehart's heart."

Lynton said, "He was returning from that mysterious trip that kept us from seeing him after we had the encounter with Susan's mother. A trip caused by his daughter. We assumed when he said that he had lost her that he meant she was dead, but she was not dead. She was just gone, maybe kidnapped, and she was nearby."

Adam stood up. "Yes, he did not even suggest she was dead. I just jumped to that conclusion. It was a logical deduction, of course, based on an assumption, an erroneous assumption. My, all these events are making no sense."

He then glanced farther down the article and blurted out, "It says all his blood was drained and he was killed on Rommel Way. That is right behind the hotel. You don't suppose..."

Lynton interrupted, "Yes, he was on his way here with some important news, no doubt."

She then turned to Susan and said, "Wily dilly discombobulated is she who deplores truth as if it were a poison."

Susan's back stiffened and she stared at Lynton with intensity. Lynton walked over to her and said, "I do not know the complete truth, but I know you are not what you seem to be."

Hesitantly and timidly, Susan sighed, but she offered no rebuttal. "Your mother," offered Lynton, "she was a Louder, but she came here from Belgium. Am I correct?"

"Yes."

"She is not your biological mother?"

"My, how did you know?"

Lynton replied, "Because I checked the birth records and the last Louder known in Belgium was in 1917, and there were no others afterwards."

"Yes, she adopted me here, when I was no more than 2 months old. She is the only mother I have ever known. I know nothing of my real parents. I was simply a waif left on the doorstep of the old parish church, and the reverend knew my mother, knew I would be in good hands."

"Maybe he thought you would be in good hands, but he was wrong. What do you remember about the visit to the Krupp estate?"

She thought long and hard, and said, "Well, I just remember that we drove into the circular driveway, and I saw some strange lights flickering inside. After that, well, I don't know. Perhaps we were there for awhile. It is a bit hazy, my recollections I mean. I just recall that we sped away and down the hillside."

LYNTON AND THE STELLENBOSCH TERROR

Sighing, Lynton said with a note of concern, "Your time there is hazy, because you want it to be. You went to see Rhinehart first, and you went there for a specific reason. Someone was there whom your mother wanted to retrieve, someone who was vital to a sinister plot that has been unfolding for a hundred years. You left with Linda." Then Lynton turned to Adam and continued, "What is Louise Rhinehart's middle name? Linda, am I right?"

"Oh my, I never thought, never realized. Yes, Louise Linda Rinehart."

"The house of Louder has an ancient history. They were known in Belgium all the way back to 900, when the family was first mentioned in the chronicles of the Strigoi, which I studied about at the University of Cape Town Library when I was working on another case in the Karoo area. I contacted a friend yesterday and he did some more research. The Louder family was known as vampire slayers or more appropriately Strigoi slayers. The Strigoi were special types of vampires, according to ancient Belgium legend. The Strigoi are thought to have two hearts and two souls and many of them can go out days or nights. They drink the blood of people in a very special way."

Adam was getting more astute now. He said, "They pierced the victims hearts and drank the blood that way rather than biting on the neck."

Smiling, Lynton said, "Smart boy. Now, my dear Adam, I shall regale you with a tale that will not top your uncanny ability to spin a yarn, but may be just as interesting. So, relax and take all this in."

The Romanian vampire myths have migrated all over the world, but these myths melded into the modern day version we read about and see in movies. However, there is a vampire legend much more sinister than the tales of Dracula, and the other terror stories about blood suckers, and it is those vampires I shall tell you about now, and I am going to piece together what will sound like a fantastic yarn that may make you shake your heads in disbelief, but I am ready to tackle something here that goes beyond mere ghosts."

Susan had a concerned look on her face, as she seemed shocked that Lynton knew so much. Her uncomfortableness did not go unnoticed by Lynton, particularly when Susan said, "We are all victims of fate. There is nothing we can do about it. That is destiny's plan. This is all nonsense about vampires, utter nonsense."

There is a great suspicion that beats deep within the mild-mannered heart of Lynton Viñas of those who proclaim that our destinies are preordained, planned by a benevolent God. Does this God plan an individual's poverty, an individual's illnesses, an individual's pain from the loss of a child, an individual's rape, an individual's murder or an individual's descent into depression? Thus she looked deliberately at Susan as she continued her explanation of something she knew Susan understood. "The Strigoi vampire myth is highly unusual, because for the most part it has been tossed into the dustbin of history. However, it was resurrected here in this little corner of South Africa, and what is known as the Stellenbosch Terror has its roots in the legend of the Strigoi. It is a tale that will, when I conclude, send cold chills up and down your spines."

Chapter 8

Kick a Hornet's Nest

She rose among us where we lay.

She swept above not far away.

We had no choice but to stay,

As a horror spread there.

Darkness shot across the sky.

Then we heard her melancholy cry;

And saw her lift white hands on high.

What shape was she who came to us,

With burning eyes so ominous,

J. WAYNE FRYE   153

LYNTON AND THE STELLENBOSCH TERROR

With fanged teeth poisonous,
And tortured face so pale?
We saw her flying to and fro,
Through the dark she did go;
Her name we did not know.

We tried to turn away; but still
As her flapping wings gave us a chill;
There in the trenches we dreamed of ill,
And dreaded the un-dead things.
Of ground red with bloody flames
Shuddering hills cracked their frames
To the foul sound of flapping wings.

Dying men there danced no tune
And cries of bitten ones stifled soon;
And over all was a blood-red moon,
Dull and nightmarish size in the skies.
We fought as commanded in all ways,
Yet everywhere we met her gaze,
Her fixed, burning yearning eyes
And our brains were mesmerized.

J. WAYNE FRYE

LYNTON AND THE STELLENBOSCH TERROR

Through the night strange music went
With voice and cry so darkly sent
We could not fathom what they meant.
Save only that they seemed
To thin the blood within our veins,
Foretelling vile, delirious pains,
And wings flapping like horrible rains.

This we heard: "Who dies for me,
He shall possess me secretly.
My terrible beauty he shall see,
And slake my body's flame.
But who denies me cursed shall be,
And slain, and buried loathsomely,
And slimed upon with shame."

And darkness fell. And like a sea
Of stumbling deaths we followed;
We who dared not stay behind.
There all night long beneath a cloud
We rose and fell, we struck and bowed.
We were the ploughman and the ploughed.

J. WAYNE FRYE   155

LYNTON AND THE STELLENBOSCH TERROR

Our eyes were red and blind as she dined.

Some, they said, touched her evil side,
Before she flapped away from us there;
And some begged her to be a bride;
And some offered themselves and died.
The trenches were now her lair,
Where men were cursed and cried,
Pleading with the gorging vampire.

She feasted on the dying and the dead,
No nectar of blood did she miss.
Small and shapely was her anointed head,
Dark and small her mouth, they said.
And lips beautiful to kiss;
Her mouth was sinister and red.
Blood in moonlight was her sweet bliss.

A thin dagger dappled bright with blood,
And the young men murdered in the bud;
And then at length the dawn
Came as hope from the east,

J. WAYNE FRYE

LYNTON AND THE STELLENBOSCH TERROR

And all that heaving horror ceased.
Silent was every bird and beast,
And the dark flapping was gone.

No word was there, no song, no bell,
No furious tongue that dreamed to tell;
Only the dead, who under her spell fell.
It was not the British who wounded men;
Causing whisperings and wails of pain
Blown slowly from the smoking plain;
It was that female vampire come again and again.

Lynton began her story. "In World War I there was a German soldier who endured the misery of trench warfare and the experiences so transformed him that he would rise up like a mighty phoenix and bring ruin to the world. Now, let me tell you about this incident and how a Strigoi wound up above the trenches that night and how a survivor of the terror saw an evil greater than any he experienced in battle. What he and a handful of survivors saw was hushed up by both sides, because it involved a terror greater than war."

LYNTON AND THE STELLENBOSCH TERROR

"First," said Lynton, "you have to know that Belgium was allied with France and Great Britain against Germany in World War I. Now, we will not fight World War I, but we will fight one battle which changed the course of the whole world as it would lead to one man believing that the occult offered Germany salvation. However, first, let me acquaint you with the Strigoi. There are many vampire legends that can be traced to the Romanians, particularly to Transylvania. The most notable legend is that of Vlad the Impaler, who was the prototype for Bram Stoker's Dracula. He was real, and he did impale his victims and it was reported that he would drink their blood. However, the myths of vampires existed long before Vlad, dating back to ancient Egypt. It was there the Strigoi legend began, when Moses was supposed to have led the Jews out of ancient Egypt, despite the fact there is no credible proof the Jews were ever even in Egypt. Nonetheless, that is not germane to what I am about to share with you."

LYNTON AND THE STELLENBOSCH TERROR

Adam shifted position, Cecile crossed her legs, and Susan had a very worried look on her face as Lynton continued. "It is written in some ancient texts that Pharaoh Osiris was the first Egyptian vampire. His brother Set had deposed him, and eventually killed him. However, Osiris was unwilling to die, and his loyal servant revived the corpse by infusing it with fresh blood fed into his heart by two small piercings with a ceremonial dagger stolen from Pharaoh Set's quarters. The dagger was called a Rapturin. It soon became apparent that a supply of blood was a necessity as long as Osiris wanted to prowl about, but if he rested for days, weeks or even months or years he did not need an inordinate supply of blood. The servant and former Pharaoh fled Egypt and settled near a place called Ypres in Belgium. There, Osiris, after an infusion of blood from several victims brought to him by his servant, was preparing a reign of terror, when he told his servant to find him a bride, and not to awaken him until the right woman was found."

"While on his mission, the servant was killed by a runaway horse that trampled him, and Osiris remained in suspended animation for 2000 years. Remember that crosses, garlic and stakes through the heart are myths used in books, because the vampire was around long before crosses, so they, in reality, would have no effect on a vampire. It makes for a good tale, but has no basis in fact. Osiris' servant had buried him in a cavern in the remote little village of Ypres, Belgium. It was there, in October of 1914 that a young girl of 16, who had lost both her parents in the war, wandered into a cave, in search of a place to hide from a great battle that was about to occur outside of the town. She progressed slowly into an alcove, and noticed lose dirt beneath her feet. She scratched on it and found a large wooden door, pulled it open and looked down upon a sarcophagus. She lowered herself into the chamber where it rested, pushed the stone covering aside, and stood in awe as she gazed down upon the perfectly preserved body of a handsome man."

LYNTON AND THE STELLENBOSCH TERROR

Lynton had the three enthralled, but, with a smile, said, "Now, I discovered this tale in an old diary at the South African National Library's rare book section in Cape Town. It was written by a discredited Egyptologist during the First World War, 1917 to be exact. His name is unimportant, but he related this story as an explanation for what occurred in the trenches one night in 1914 when the aforementioned soldier was so adversely affected that he would embrace the occult and initiate a horror that would engulf almost the entire world. Stay with me and I shall lead you on a frightful journey into a world of evil."

"It was Osiris there perfectly preserved, and it so happened that the girl had a slight cut on her lip, and as she leaned over the coffin, a drop of blood fell onto Osiris' lips. The elixir of life was the taste he had waited for so long, and he savoured it as the young girl stood dumbstruck in terror. Still, she was so mesmerized that she could not move, as Osiris reached up and pulled her down to him, kissing her."

"He lured her through hypnotic powers to lie beside him with the promise of immortality. Now, if a vampire thirsts for blood only, he drinks the elixir like a man dying of thirst in the desert who comes upon an oasis where water is abundant. However, if you want to turn someone into a vampire, you must drink the blood of the victim slowly over a period of time. Osiris had decided to make this woman his bride, but remember that Osiris was a Strigoi vampire, so he had to have blood from the heart, and to prepare the heart, according to tradition, he had to gently pierce it with a Rapturin. But, of course, it was in the ceremonial chest next to his coffin. He commanded her to bring it to him. He pierced her heart and over a period of days, he drank the elixir of life very slowly while making sure she was not losing too much blood, so that he could use her in his quest for more blood that would reinvigorate him, and make him into a strong Strigoi again, so that he might ravage the countryside at will to satisfy his growing thirst for blood."

LYNTON AND THE STELLENBOSCH TERROR

Susan appeared very uncomfortable as Lynton continued. "War is an abomination where the poor are sent to die while the privileged are kept safe. In today's world, war is a capitalist venture that brings great financial rewards to a few while the many are sacrificed for the glory of greed. In World War I, although not as pronounced as it is today, the poor were sent out to be slaughtered while the industrial class reaped huge financial rewards. Thus, this aforementioned common soldier, being from the poor class, was relegated to be cannon fodder in the trenches outside Ypres, Belgium."

"As the poor soldier was readying for battle, in that cavern, Osiris was preparing his bride to do his bidding. Within a few days, she was under his complete control. There are instances when all the stars seem to be aligned and things just fall into place. As the young woman told of the preparation for a great battle, Osiris imagined all that human flesh out in the open as a grand opportunity for him to feast almost at will."

"What is reported is not always the entire story of what happened, because the truth can have an adverse effect on the efforts of governments to control the populaces and keep them in lock-step with supporting nations that are morally bankrupt. In those trenches and in the fields were over five million German soldiers, and one of them was the aforementioned private, who would survive what was the single most terrible night ever experienced by German soldiers, and it was not the battle itself that was so horrible, but the carnage wrought on one isolated unit of about twenty thousand men that would only be whispered about, because the truth was too horrible to reveal, as it would have caused wide-spread panic, and maybe have impeded the war effort. Because over five million German soldiers were spread across the front confronting four and one-half million French, British and Belgium soldiers, the killed and wounded were so numerous that what happened in one area of the battlefield was forever lost to history."

LYNTON AND THE STELLENBOSCH TERROR

Lynton was regaling the three with precision, and continued as they all eagerly waited for more of the harrowing tale. "Thus, this one lone soldier was part of the assault battalion which was going to attack the British, French and Belgium lines in the dead of night. The men climbed over the top, running toward the enemy lines with fury in their eyes. As the rat-a-tat-tat of machine gun fire and sparkling tracers lit up the dark while mortars exploded across the battlefield blowing men to smithereens, suddenly, there across the sky in the dense dark of the night, flapping across the dull, cloud covered quarter moon was a giant bat. It was so huge that it nearly blotted out what little light there was from the moon. It swooped down upon men who were not dead, but lay wounded on the battlefield. A gruesome, blood curdling sound could be heard in the darkness as men screamed. A thin blade could be seen rising and falling in a rhythmic nature from one area to the other, and the screams of agony were pounding into this one soldier's head."

"After a few minutes, the bat raised itself in swift fashion from the battlefield and flew off time and again with screaming men in its clutches. A short time later, it returned with another bat and the feasting continued unabated hour after hour. The soldier I mentioned took aim at the bats and shot, knowing he had hit them, but they did not fall. They were impervious to shot and shell. This went on until the dawn, when, with the creeping of the sun above the horizon, the bats swiftly flew off with wings flapping so loud they seemed to make the ground vibrate from the intensity."

"That night, of the 20,000 men, over 19,000 were killed, but when the survivors told of what happened with the bats, the commanders would not believe them. That lone soldier, who had shot at the bats, pleaded for one captain to examine some of the dead men. Many had died from gunshots and mortar shells, but hundreds had only minor wounds that should not have killed them, but they had their combat fatigues ripped open, and over their hearts were two puncture wounds and they were void of any blood; it having apparently been sucked out by the two bats. What occurred was hushed up by the military authorities, but that soldier carried the horror of that night forever. He recorded the event in a dairy that was discovered years ago by a professor. That soldier would go on to believe in the power of the occult, and he would call upon its power as he rose to great prominence in Germany after World War I. This man's name was Adolph Hitler."

All there were in shock, but Lynton was not through weaving her tale. She continued. "Throughout most of the rest of the war, German, British, French, Belgium and even American troops reported incidents in Belgium where two bats would descend upon battlefields and drink the blood of soldiers who were dying. It was always just one or two bats, and they could absolutely not be killed by bullets."

"Then in August of 1917, something strange happened. The munitions firm of Krupp Industries, which had made the famous Big Bertha artillery piece, sent Myron Krupp, a distant cousin of the company's president to locate a special type of mineral in the caves around Ypres, as they were going to develop a precursor to atomic fusion and use the element to fuse a shell of immense power. Fortunately, or unfortunately, depending on how you look at it, the mineral was never found, and Myron Krupp announced he was moving to South Africa at the height of the war."

Adam said, "That was the Krupp who moved to Kleingeluk and built that castle-like structure on the hillside."

"Correct, and my guess is that he brought the sarcophagus of Osiris with him, and probably a new sarcophagus for Osiris' mate. The place appears to have been abandoned, but it is not, never has been, because within those walls are the crypts of vampires." Then Lynton turned to Susan and said, "I am not here in this hotel in search of a ghost. Rather, I am on the trail of vampires. The one ghost you people are seeing has no ill intent. It is here to warn people of danger."

LYNTON AND THE STELLENBOSCH TERROR

"What," proclaimed Adam?

"Yes, the apparition seen by Harold all those years ago was not of evil intent. It was there to try and warn him, warn him that his wife and children were intended victims of cultists, who were making sacrifices to Osiris and his wife, two vampires that were residing at the Krupp estate. In this hotel, there is a ghost and a visiting vampire. One is good and the other evil." She turned to Adam's mother and continued. "You grandmother was a servant to evil, the evil of a vampire. She killed the professor to keep him from uncovering what was going on. The vampire was what people considered a ghost. It is he who roams about here in this hotel, but he is not confined here, nor is the other entity, which is the spirit of the professor."

She looked over at Adam. "Both entities are cloaked figures. So, they are sometimes confused, but the professor's spirit often wanders about just as he was before he was killed. Apparently, he sometimes roams about as the professor, seen only by those psychically attuned."

"Wait," interjected Adam. "You have seen him."

"I have, twice, and both times you did not see him. He is a bald, slightly stooped shoulder middle aged man, who does not utter a word, only greets me with a nod as he walks down the hallway, unnoticed by you, of course."

"Oh my," offered Cecile. "What are we to do?"

"I am not sure. The vampire is the cloaked figure you have encountered, but usually before he shows up, the kind entity, the professor, also in a dark cloak, the one encountered by Harold all those years ago, and maybe seen by others who were ultimately killed, tries to issue a warning, but it is incapable of speech."

Adam, rising and walking over to the window, looked out, then turned and said, "How do we know which one is which?"

"I am not sure. I do know that I awoke on the floor one night, and I believe that I was ready to be sacrificed, but the good entity somehow intervened and saved me. Later I found the letter opener with blood on it, no doubt my own."

Adam said, "But how and why does that dagger always wind up back in that room?"

"The how is easy. It is put there by Osiris after he prowls for blood. Why is more problematic, but I do have an idea. However," and then she looked over at Susan, who had remained quiet, and said, "You, my dear, can provide the details on the why. For example, I know that Linda, who was Eric Rhinehart's daughter, was in that car for a reason, and your mother had stopped by Eric's and the Krupp estate, for specific reasons. Am I right?"

Susan took a deep breath. "Yes, we went to Eric's because Linda was thought to be the reincarnation of Osiris' sister. Linda, under the influence of my mother told her father she could never return to him. The two men with us had to restrain him from attacking my mother. He was held down, brutally assaulted and left unconscious as we pulled away with Linda, who was completely under my mother's control. We were headed for a rendezvous with destiny, a destiny foretold in ancient Egypt."

Lynton interrupted. "From Geb, the sky god, and Nut, the earth goddess came four children: Osiris, Isis, Set and Nepthys. Osiris was the oldest and so became king of Egypt, but was killed by his brother, Set. Osiris was married to his sister Isis when he was killed. She became one of Set's wives afterward, not out of love, but out of survival instinct. Now, Osiris has found her again, reincarnated, he believes, in the body of Linda Rhinehart. However, he is already married to someone, the girl who discovered him in Ypres. He plans to find his sister a mate, which is why he sent some of his devotees, one of which is your mother, my dear Susan, to kidnap her, and prepare her for marriage?"

Susan nodded affirmatively, as Lynton continued. "She has been under Osiris' spell for awhile, as he and his mate have been slowly drinking her blood, preparing her to become a vampire. Your mother was taking her to find a mate, but first she was taken to the Krupp estate for a final blood letting."

"She was, yes. She was with us, of course, I can only assume, because I was apparently in a hypnotic state while we were there, as I do not remember what happened."

"Susan, it is time for the deception to stop. You were not hypnotised at the Krupp estate. In fact, you were not injured at all, you were sent here to spy on us, as an agent of Osiris. You were not kidnapped from your room that night either. You had gone back to the Krupp estate, where your mother had summoned you, and there you observed Linda being married, and joining what was perceived by those there to be her brother Osiris and his bride in a coven of evil. Whom did she marry? I know it had to be someone from Stellenbosch. It is time for you to stop your deception."

"I did not see. He was covered in a dark cloak and made his way to an altar where he stood as the two were joined as one in an ancient ritual of marriage between the Strigoi," offered an unconvincing Susan.

Lynton said, "We now have four Strigoi to deal with, and other evil ones that are their minions, as they are serving in hopes that Osiris will reward them with the slow blood letting that will guarantee them immortality."

Adam took a deep breath and said, "I brought you into a hornet's nest of evil my dear Lynton."

Lynton smiled and said, "I am the girl who loves to kick a hornet's nest!"

Chapter 9

Worse Than a Ghost or a Vampire – Me

Piercing hearts where death ran

As in a blood-letting river,

The dye of death never faded.

Blinding worship of wickedness,

And Osiris for eternity forgot to die,

As the dragons of evil were on the fly

And brought destruction across the land.

The next day with an elastic step, inhaling the morning-air with voluptuous delight, Lynton made her way down the main street, and lying stretched out before her, bathed in light and pulsating with life was a new day that she welcomed with delight, putting the madness of the night behind her. On the street, her magnetic power compelled recognition, and she stepped through the midst of the crowd with her usual determined stride that hailed someone who was self-confident and dedicated to a cause. After walking a block or two, she suddenly halted before a jeweller's shop. Arrayed in the window were priceless gems that shone in the glare like mystical serpent-eyes, green, pomegranate and water-blue. And as she stood there, the dazzling radiance before her was transformed in the prism of her mind into something great and very wonderful that might, some day, be a poem. Then her attention was diverted by a small group of native girls merrily dancing on the sidewalk. She joined the circle of amused spectators, to watch those bits of femininity swaying airily to and fro in unison with the tune of the jangling bells tied to their dainty young ankles.

LYNTON AND THE STELLENBOSCH TERROR

One girl of maybe 14 especially attracted her notice, a slim very animated girl with hair dishevelled and feet hardly touching the ground. She suggested an orange-leaf dancing on a sunbeam. As a former dancer, for several minutes Lynton followed with keen delight her gracefulness, but suddenly the girl glanced into her eyes and a wicked look ensued as she pointed directly at her and for a split second, fanged teeth were displayed. Lynton shook her head as if to loosen the image, and, indeed it was gone as afterward the girl was just smiling at her. She turned to her left and continued her stroll, seemingly without aim; in reality she followed, with nervous intensity, the multiform undulations of the populace and several people seemed to, for a split second, have faces that exhibited fanged teeth and piercing red eyes. Again she shook her head and the images were gone.

As she strolled along, beside her appeared a familiar figure, the constable who had come to Room 227. He said, "Good morning, Ms. Viñas."

Recognizing him, she said, "And good morning to you constable."

His friendly reply seemed to almost mock her. "Herbert please, Ms. Viñas, Herbert Manly."

"Lynton, please."

"Sure, and what brings you out this fine morning, Lynton?"

"Just a morning constitutional."

"Lovely day for it. I guess you are surprised by the scourge of murder that has overwhelmed this town since your arrival?"

"Is that an observation or an indictment, Herbert?"

"Observational, of course, but I have googled you, and your investigational prowess is well-documented."

"Well, don't believe everything you read on the internet. Embellishment is the norm there I am afraid."

"I do not think in your case it is embellishment, but I should warn you that interfering with a police investigation is a serious offence."

LYNTON AND THE STELLENBOSCH TERROR

Lynton stopped at the intersection, turned to her right to cross, and purposefully made it plain their walk was over, as she turned her head left, stared directly at Constable Manly and said, "I will keep that in mind, and I shall also keep in mind that in most countries, and I am sure in South Africa also, it is a crime for a policeman to try and intimidate someone."

As she crossed the street, she never looked back, but the constable's eyes were staring with intensity, and they were not staring at the cute wiggle from side to side as her hips swayed in their customary hypnotic fashion. The sway that could slay was having no effect on him.

She thought of the Krupp mansion on the hill, and of Susan and how she had crept out and gone there. And that night on the bridge, when the car overturned, Countess Louder was not on her way out of town but had intentionally crossed that bridge for a specific reason at a specific time. The accident, itself, was not planned but was indeed fortuitous.

Eric Rhinehart had thought they went to town with his daughter in tow, but he was on a wild goose chase, and came back to spy on the Krupp Estate. Then, when he was coming to see Adam with news of what was going on, he was brutally slain. Why did he not go to the police and tell them what was happening to his daughter?

Lynton strolled about town for a long time just going over in her mind all that occurred. She had lunch at Mussel Monger Oyster Bar around 2:00 PM, and sat there until 4 enjoying the ambiance as she tried to tie things together in an extremely complicated set of affairs. Looking down at her stomach, she realized she was eating too much and decided for another stroll to try and work off some of the excess calories. She walked and walked, finally stopping at the Botanical Gardens where she sat until the sun began to disappear in the distance.

She walked back to the hotel perplexed and worried about what her next step would be. She did not have to wait long to decide. As she strolled in, Constable Manly was at the reception desk talking to Cecile Kruger. When Lynton meandered up, he greeted her with a nod. Lynton knew why he was there. She said, "No, I am not checking out. I am not leaving until I am ready, and you can try to get immigration to revoke my visa if you want, but good luck. I have a lawyer friend in Cape Town, and he will tie it up in court. You had better leave me alone and spend your time chasing a killer, rather than harassing a little Filipino girl who will not cower before your arrogance. My guess is some powerful forces want me out of here, and it is they you serve."

"You had better watch your step little girl," replied Constable Manly.

Smiling Lynton said, "I always watch my step; otherwise, you never know what you might step in. And it appears I have stepped into a cover-up of evil. I am going up to my room and you can tell the rich, the privileged and powerful whom you serve rather than the people you should be serving, that they had better watch where they are stepping.

LYNTON AND THE STELLENBOSCH TERROR

I am here to stay, and you said you looked me up on the internet, so you know about my intense determination that dispatched other miscreants of mayhem other times in other places. So, you better warn people who want me gone that I am about to put on my justice shoes and they will be clicking a tune of danger as I prance about in search of answers, and I'll deliver a blow of retribution to anyone who gets between me and the truth."

Lynton winked at Cecile, turned her back to a dumbfounded, speechless Constable Manly and headed up the stairs with a confident stride that spoke of stubbornness born in determination.

She flopped down on her bed, stared at the ceiling and tried to control her seething anger. She hated authority that stood against justice in a world where the mighty ruled with impunity. There were some good law enforcement officers, but far too many of them over the years in service to the moneyed class had forgotten that the poor, the unprivileged and the marginalized had been sacrificed at the altar of greed and privilege to serve the few at the expense of the many. The world was not a very pleasant place for those who floundered in a sea of misery trying to keep their heads above water in an evil system that catered only to those at the top of the economic ladder, and to those who offered a titillating reward for service to evil.

Lynton lay staring at the ceiling as the moon was covered by a cloud, bathing the room in darkness. She waited, waited for one of the cloaked figures to manifest itself. Good or evil entity, she was going to confront it.

Upon the invitingly comfortable mattress Lynton lay in quiet contemplation. She looked to her right, and the dagger-like letter opener was not there. She opened the drawer. It was not there either.

The streetlights filtering through the slightly parted curtains shed a faint illumination in the room, just enough for Lynton to see a cloaked figure morphing through the door and slowly gliding her way. She felt a disagreeable sensation of cold. Still, she was determined not to cower in fear, as she was prepared to confront the entity on her terms, but first wanted to let it fully manifest itself and reveal its intentions.

Manifestation was a slow process as it was, at first, more outline and transparency than solid matter. Standing at the foot of her bed, it began to take on form of a more pronounced nature. She had moved both pillows under her head, so she was elevated enough for a good view of the thing. She began to feel an even more intense cold as a gust of wind filtered across her face. The figure slowly rose, floated upward in an upright position off the floor until its feet were level with the footboard. It was completely covered with a thick black cloak and slowly began to move to a straight alignment with head angled over the bed and feet rising as it floated above.

Still, Lynton doubted her senses, and was now breathing heavily. Her eyes were riveted on the figure floating above her bed. She could not see the face as the hood of the cloak completely covered it, but she could see its eyes that were fiery red and glowing brilliantly. This was no vampire. It was something ghostly, but it was making no aggressive moves whatsoever, only floating above the bed. It was like the body of a man long dead, and yet it moved, and the dead fiery eyes seemed to stare pleadingly at her out of the darkness.

The thing paused an instant, hovering over her prostrate body, and she could have screamed, but there was a serenity in the entity that seemed to let her know that there was no ill intent. It's pleading eyes were more intense and Lynton suddenly knew who the entity was. She sit up in the bed, never taking her eyes off it and said, "I will follow you, professor."

The entity floated toward the door and morphed through it. Lynton opened the door and went into the hallway. There, floating just below the ceiling was the entity and it was moving toward Room 228, where Susan slept. Lynton hurried down the stairs to the front desk and said to Adam, who was on duty. "Keys to 228, now."

Adam started to say something, but before he could utter a word, Lynton said, "Not now."

He handed her the keys and the two of them bounded up the stairs. When they got to the hallway, the entity was gone. Lynton inserted the key and the two of them burst into the room. Susan lay on the bed naked, and as Lynton rushed in, Adam flipped on the lights. Over her heart were two small indentations, and she was breathing in a strained matter. Adam said, "I'll call a doctor."

Susan shouted, "No, please don't. No doctors."

It was then that from behind the door, Constable Manly magically appeared. Had he been behind the door when they entered the room? Was he a pervert spying on the naked Susan? No, definitely not thought Lynton, as she began to comprehend the real reason he was there, a reason that she would make evident to Adam later on.

"Why Constable Manly," offered Lynton, "you do seem to pop up at the most opportune times. Is voyeurism a part of your job?"

Susan seemed discombobulated by what was going on as she put on her robe. She said, "What happened to me?"

Manly said, "You were apparently attacked. Can you tell me by whom?"

"I can tell you nothing," replied Susan as she stared at Manly. "I came to my room, lay down, started to read, and suddenly the room light went out and that is the last I remember."

Then she quickly added, "Except, there was an interruption. Yes, I know that because I awakened for a split second, and I remember a dark figure leaning over me, and then another dark figure over by the door, seeming to float through it. Whatever or whoever was leaning over me disappeared. I remember hearing wings flapping. Yes, huge wings from the sounds of it."

Manly looked at Lynton and Adam, and Cecile, who had entered the room. "Absolute poppycock, utter nonsense."

Lynton said, "The nonsense is what you were doing in this room."

Manly replied, "You woman need to get out of Stellenbosch before you find yourself on a slab in the morgue."

Lynton, perturbed now, said, "You think you are fooling me?" Then she looked over at Susan and continued, "I am not the fool either of you think I am. You invited whoever or whatever was here into this room. Susan, you are an enigma."

Manly walked over directly in front of Lynton and said, "Woman, I have had about enough of you, and I will only tolerate your belligerence for so long." He then, looked in a very recognizable way at Susan while he walked to the door. As he was leaving, he looked back at Lynton and said, "I am about to bring you down you arrogant little bitch."

Lynton smiled and said, "Manly, there is something worse to deal with than a ghost or a vampire – me!"

Chapter 10

End This Terror

Foul Demons of the night hide the light.

Lord Byron once told of a vampire's lair

And how there went a maiden fair.

Vampires smelling of death are sent,

Corpses shall from their tombs be rent.

Foul Demons of the night hide the light.

Ghastly haunting a native place

To suck the blood of any race;

There from any daughter, sister or wife,

LYNTON AND THE STELLENBOSCH TERROR

At midnight to drain the stream of life.

Foul Demons of the night hide the light,
Yet loathe the banquet which perforce
Must feed the livid living corpse.
The victims in ecstasy expire,
Knowing the demon for their sire.

Foul Demons of the evil hide the light,
Vampires all embracing the night,
Flapping their wings in sinister flight.
But Lynton Viñas is on the prowl
To bring down vampires most foul.

Susan looked up at Lynton and said, "You don't trust me?"

"I trust that there was a vampire visiting here, and the ghost of the professor came in to confront it, just as it has done in my room, trying to save me, as it has tried to save so many over the years."

Adam looked at Lynton. "It is the professor."

"It is. He is the same one who warned Harold and all the others. Osiris appears in 227 before killing. He procures the Rapturin. The thing seen leaning over the bodies of all those killed is not evil. It is good. It tried to prevent the terror, but it has not the power of speech. All it can do is warn as a spectre. Somehow it can manifest itself on occasion in daylight as it did twice with me right out there in the hallway."

Adam said, "But what of the dagger. Why does it keep being brought back to that room?"

Lynton looked over at Susan and said, "You know why don't you?"

Closing her eyes momentarily, and then opening them while sighing, she almost arrogantly replied, "Yes, of course."

Lynton with that little mischievous smile she gets when she has figured out a mystery said, "The dagger must be placed either in or on the desk, because that desk is a covering for something far more sinister, something that has been hidden in it, very artfully hidden for many years."

Susan, shocked that Lynton was so perceptive, said, "How did you know?"

"It was easy. All I did was google ceremonial daggers used in the ritual of the world's first Strigoi vampire. It said that the daggers had to be placed, when not in use, on or in a very special sacrificial chest. The lids of most Egyptian chests were hinged, but mostly the cover was completely removed when the chest was opened. Flanges or pegs glued to the lids and inserted into appropriate holes in the chests' walls kept them in place. In order to lock the chests, strings were tied to knobs on the lids and sealed with clay seals. I examined that stand by the bed in 227, and it is easy to discern that it is a covering for another chest. Beneath that covering is an ancient Egyptian desk that was first brought to Belgium when Osiris had his servant bring his body there, along with the ceremonial chest that housed the dagger, the Rapturin. It was in that cave when his body was discovered by the young girl who released terror on the battlefield."

Susan sighed and nodded her head affirmatively as Lynton turned to Cecile, who had entered the room, and Adam. She was very precise with her words to them. "Strangers have offered to buy that desk in Room 227 off and on for years haven't they, but you never sold it, and your grandmother was its keeper. It was she who maintained the sanctity of the sacrificial chest for so long."

"My grandmother, yes. I can remember her always obsessively protecting that chest, always being concerned about it, and yes, in the past, several people have asked to buy it. You think they wanted it so they could bring it to the Krupp Estate, where it would be more convenient for the Strigoi to use it for blood letting."

Ever the philosophical sage, Lynton said, "Escaping malignant wickedness is not easy in a world where the evil of economic inequity is embraced and sanctified by governments that only serve those at the top of the economic ladder. Evil is the real religion of the world, because even those who call themselves Christian, Muslim or whatever bow before the evil of greed. Those people at the Krupp estate are all wealthy in perverse evil and the evil of money worship is not enough for them. They want to become immortal, even if it is done by sacrificing the living, because they believe they are entitled. Those people reek of evil, seethe with the imperfections of the real sins of the world, the sins of envy, gluttony, greed, lust, pride and using their wrath to subject others in their feeding frenzy on the blood of the living to insure their immortality. Escaping that is not easy, and people line up to embrace this evil, because we all are far too self-indulgent." She then turned to Susan and continued. "I cannot free you from this evil Susan, only you can do that, but I will help you all I possibly can."

Lynton looked into Susan's eyes as she continued, "You all saw those pictures. The countess Louder is not human." Not taking her eyes off Susan, who displayed a look of intense concern, Lynton sighed and said, "Now, we go into the lair of the Strigoi and end this terror."

Chapter 11

Into a Deep Slumber

Huge blocks of granite rise into the air

As intrepid demon fighter Lynton will prepare.

In the Krupp estate on high,

Gilded gargoyle statues stand by.

There is evil in a secret lair.

Darkness dances to death there.

Flapping bat wings crown the sky;

As life-blood throbs, the fevered pulses fly.

Immense, defiant, breathless evil seethes fair,

And ever listens in the ceaseless din,

LYNTON AND THE STELLENBOSCH TERROR

Waiting for victims who shall come.
The vampire lips shall boldly claim their own,
And render sonant what in all becomes numb,
The splendour, the madness and the sin
In nightmares of forged iron and hard stone.

The culmination of most vampire hunts ends in a vampire's lair, but often such locales hold nothing but emptiness, especially in the case of Strigoi, as their coffins are found in places well hidden from prying eyes, and as Lynton mapped out with her determined comrades a method for getting into the lair that was on the hillside in Kleingeluk, an obvious question was asked by Adam: "First, how do we kill these creatures?"

"I called my professor friend at the University of Cape Town, who happens to be a firm non-believer in such fantastic creatures, but he is an expert on them nonetheless. The two hearts in the Strigoi are the only method of death to it. Driving a stake through the hearts is not effective on a Strigoi. The two hearts must be removed and each cut in half, then burned and buried. Remember that crosses, garlic, all the tried and true methods used in books and movies are superfluous manifestations of creative minds. We are dealing here with creatures that function in day and night, but they do sometimes rest during daylight. The days are primarily reserved for the servants of the Strigoi, who serve them in hopes of obtaining immortality. The only protection for us is to go into the lair after these creatures during daylight and hope they are at rest. Only then are we safe from them, but not safe from their servants who are sworn to protect their lairs from all intruders who defy the sanctuaries of the Strigoi."

Lynton turned to Susan and said, "The two men with you the night of the crash are not Strigoi yet. Am I right?"

"Yes. It is a long, tedious process but the reward is immortality. However, what you pay for that immortality is the death of your conscience, the end of compassion for your fellow man."

"How many people Susan were at the estate the night you disappeared?"

"There was. Let me see, "Osiris and his mate.""

Lynton interrupted her, "And you can say it now Susan, his mate is your mother. Am I right?"

Bowing her head, she whispered, "Yes."

Cecile and Adam stood in shock as Lynton said, "It was she who was the young girl at Ypres, and discovered Osiris' lair in Belgium. The picture you saw was not a relative, but she. The countess has not aged, because she became through Osiris, a Strigoi. And yes, you can take a picture of a Strigoi and despite what you have seen in movies, you can see their reflections in a mirror."

Susan said, "Yes, you are correct in all you say Lynton, but even I cannot explain why I am the living image of that girl in the picture we all saw."

With a bewildered look, Lynton said, "Nor can I at this point. However, we must still know how many Strigoi we are dealing with. How many we must defeat. We need to know the total number so we can get them all."

"As I said, Osiris, my mother, Linda, who may or may not be completely morphed into a Strigoi at this point, and the other cloaked figure there whom I do not know, but he may not be completely transformed either."

"So," said Lynton, "we are dealing with two for-sure Strigoi, maybe four including the other two who may or may not be transformed yet, and the two male servants. Let's get ready to kick some demon butt."

The four prepared for their journey at sunrise with no trepidation apparent, as they were determined to end the Stellenbosch terror. However, as Lynton lay down, setting her alarm so she would awaken at sunrise to go into battle, she stared at the ceiling, reflecting on all that had led to this point. Meanwhile, Adam quietly walked up the stairs, entered the hallway, and walked to Room 228, where he listened for no apparent reason at Susan's door. He was heartbroken.

Leaning his ear against the door, he heard the muffled sounds of a man, and he instantly knew who it was. Why was she meeting Constable Manly? He bowed his head, turned and despondently went back downstairs, wondering how she could find such a despicable man appealing.

Lynton's room was bathed in darkness except for the moonlight which was flickering slightly through the closed curtains. Instinctively, she looked to her right at the chest next to the bed and reached over to pull out the drawer. The Rapturin was still there, so there would be no blood lust this night. Then, she saw something ominous at the foot of the bed; a dark shadow began to form. She was not afraid. She sat up in the bed and said, "Whatever you are I wish you would speak. I know you have no ill intent, for you have spent years trying to warn people of danger. What is it you want me to know?"

The entity began to take complete form in the usual way, and she was almost tempted to leap up and rip that hood off and confront it face to face – woman to entity. She restrained herself though and just waited for whatever its next action would be. Gradually it began to very deliberately rise above the foot-board, floating ever so slowly toward the ceiling. She lay back down as it adjusted itself into a perpendicular position, hovering over her with eyes seeming to bore into her eyes and suddenly she felt a wave of horror as black and white images began flickering like an old movie on the ceiling above her.

She was in the trenches as a battle raged furiously about her. She realized she was in Ypres, Belgium and as men were falling under shot and shell she could hear their anguished cries. The agony caused tears to form in her eyes, and then she saw that lone moustached soldier again, the one who had been so tempered by battle that he became a monster who engulfed the world in war twenty years later. Then the two bats descended from the dark sky and began feasting on the wounded, and she knew what the entity was trying to reveal when the two bats swept into the trench as the soldier willingly lay down in the filth and slime waiting for the Rapturin to pierce his now exposed chest and the blood lust began in earnest as he welcomed it with glee. The images faded to black, but as quickly as they were gone, they came back again as another battle was raging, and again the bats descended from the dark skies as the same soldier lay in the trench, waiting for their blood letting. It was all becoming clear now. She blinked her eyes and the images and the entity were gone.

The coming day's battle preying on her mind, she kept tossing and turning, as she knew not what to expect. She had been in the lions' dens of evil many times before, and she had stood toe-to-toe with the vilest of demons and emerged triumphant. Still, there was something about all this that she felt she was overlooking, a link that would perhaps tie together the various elements of this most perplexing mystery. Of course, there was also the mystery of why Susan bore such a striking resemblance to the girl in the picture, and even carried the same birthmark.

Meanwhile, in another place, the vampires' sarcophagi were side by side on stone pedestal stands in the centre of a room deep in the bowels of the Krupp estate. A red velvet cloth blanketed the pedestal. Exotic and esoteric symbols decorated the cloth's hem. Several plush rugs covered the floor. Under each lay an ironbound trapdoor. Beneath each trapdoor lay a narrow but deep, rough-hewn ornamental oubliette. The bloodless remains of several random victims were strewn all about. The rotting, decomposing corpses fouled the air of this den of inequity with a putrid smell that made mortals want to vomit, but was as sweet as the smell of roses to the Strigoi and their servants.

Tapestries covered the walls of the chamber. Some had been defaced and slashed in fits of fury, no doubt by former vampire hunters who had failed in their mission to eradicate these despicable beings. These poor vampire hunters were tortured for defiling the evil sanctuary of these creatures and had been pinned to the far wall by spears thrust through their hands and feet in mock crucifixions. Additionally, each had a wooden stake driven through their mouths at just the right angle which would not have killed them but caused excruciating pain as they slowly died.

Behind the sarcophagi was a giant wall and a huge iron door. Behind the door lay the vampires spare coffins in case a hasty trip to another locale might be required. A giant black book stood on an ornate desk with Pharaohonic symbols along with an ancient fine quill pen and a pot of ink. The book, written in hieroglyphic script called mdju netje (words of the gods) listed the vampires' more memorable victims in random order and provided details of how they were stalked and killed. The stalking was almost as pleasurable as the killing, as the fear brought these creatures great joy.

Grizzly trophies taken from the bloodless corpses of the victims were piled in one corner of the huge room. The items included a baby's rattle, tiny pyjamas, a hand-sewn bonnet, false teeth, bras, panties and purses. Then, all piled up to one side were several blood-stained crucifixes and piles of garlic, no doubt, used by foolish vampire hunters who were unaware they were dealing with Strigoi.

An ornate wardrobe of dark-stained wood dominated the other far corner of the room, as even vampires like an occasional change of their dark hooded robes that envelope their bodies.

Probably, much to the chagrin of the uninformed, a large, ornate mirror hung from one wall. Yes, the Strigoi can see their images and they love to prance about in front of the mirror and gaze upon themselves as they prepare for the hunt.

A row of five heavy iron manacles was set into one wall. None of the sets was currently occupied, but specks of dried blood covered the surrounding walls and floor, indicating that making potential victims squirm in fear was an enjoyable pastime for the Strigoi.

A portrait covered by a blood red cloth hung on a nearby wall. Behind that cloth was the portrait that portrayed how a single vampire rose from ashes to join the two hosts who feasted on the soldiers who had ravaged the battlefield in a feeding frenzy. This was the vampire born of battle, shot and shell to corral all the evil imaginable and prepare the world for a reign of terror like it had never known. In the eyes of this evil one there was a rapturous joy that embraced pure wickedness. Never has there been a portrait of so much evil. In the end, it was a likeness that would shock and awe all who gazed upon it, for it harboured the surprise of the ages, an evil that all thought had died long ago, but still lived to one day lead a revolt of repulsiveness and engulf the world in flames. Only the little brown meek girl lying on her bed in room 227 stood between this evil and total chaos. She drifted off to sleep not knowing that as one entity had left her room, another entered as it was night and at night the vampire comes to grasp that ceremonial Rapturin and rain down evil upon the unsuspecting. She lay there rhythmically breathing, as the evil entity opened the drawer, removed the dagger, leaned over her, pulled back the sheet and gazed at her naked body.

LYNTON AND THE STELLENBOSCH TERROR

There was no sexual arousal, only the arousal of evil which beat in both hearts of this abomination there in room 227. He raised the Rapturin and gently pricked two small openings between her breasts, then placed it back on the table. He started to bend down to enjoy the elixir of immortality that would end the dogged pursuit by the dynamic dynamo. As his fanged teeth were within a few centimetres of the two tiny puncture wounds, Lynton's eyes opened. Realizing that her predicament could not be assuaged by a scream, she reached to her right, where the dagger had been placed on the table, grasped it in her right hand and thrust it into the left arm of the creature. A shrill scream resounded all about the room and the entity rose upward, floating above the bed.

It spoke in German some obvious unintelligible profanities to Lynton. The hood covering its head made it impossible to see its face. As it started to zoom back down upon her, she rolled off the bed, grabbed the lamp by the left bedside table and ripped the shade off, flipping on the one light at night which is effective in warding off Strigoi, a florescent bulb, because it gives off UV rays similar to the sun. She held it in front of her with the assuredness her Cape Town professor friend was right in urging her to put in a fluorescent bulb to ward off Strigoi. The evil abomination fluttered about a few seconds, again mumbling something in German, transformed itself to a huge bat and flew rapidly out the window into the darkness.

Lynton struggled to her feet, exhausted and panting heavily. She flopped on the bed face down and lay there thankful she had the forethought to learn how to ward off a Strigoi with penetrating florescent light. She rolled over on her back and stared up at the ceiling hoping there would be no more manifestations. She took a deep breath and fell into a deep slumber.

Chapter 12

The Home Where Evil Had Come to Dwell

Tonight she treads the unsubstantial way

That looms before her, as the thundering night

Falls all about so vampires can have their say.

She is armed with wits for the bitter fight,

Bringing flames of indignation for this noble goal.

These are signs that must be read;

Her sword is the fervour of her soul

Levelled against those by warm blood fed.

The darkness beckons: she has gone,

Before this terrible hour towards the gloom.

LYNTON AND THE STELLENBOSCH TERROR

She braves the wild dragon, calls the tiger on
With whirling cries of pride, seeking the tomb
Where vampires battened with wills of steel
Have wrought evil through gates of death.
Lynton, demon fighter supreme, hath the will
To fight these vile creatures to her last breath.

Lynton's slumber was not interrupted by any more manifestations of entities in room 227, and that night, with the dagger safely stowed away, no murders were committed, at least, in the city proper, but what was going on elsewhere was indeterminable. She knew that even without the Rapturin, the Strigoi still needed fresh blood for survival, and although the ritual was important to their ultimate well-being, they could kill without it, kill just for the necessity of feeding their appetite for survival.

Lynton's sleep was restless, as she kept reflecting on what she had seen flickering on the ceiling. What was that good entity trying to warn her about? Was there something she had not figured on ominously waiting at the Krupp estate?

LYNTON AND THE STELLENBOSCH TERROR

When Lynton went down for breakfast to join Susan, Cecile and Adam; there at the table, helping himself to waffles and orange juice, was the constable. He looked pale and drawn, as if he, like Lynton had a restless night. He greeted her with a slight snarl across his lips, as he said, "Anything bother you in your room last night?"

Lynton, not liking him even more now, replied, "Would it make any difference if something did bother me?"

He got a scowl on his face. "Frankly, I don't give a damn, but there was an attack on a dozen sheep last night in Kleingeluk. Had all their blood drained apparently, according to the vet, before they were dead. All died from a loss of blood. Maybe it was that vampire you people seem to think is prowling around as it also likes lamb."

Lynton interjected, "Not vampire, vampires."

A slight smile crossed his lips as he replied, "Oh, so now we have a whole bevy of these creatures of the night out killing sheep as well as people. I thought vampires only bit people."

Lynton leaned forward and directed her remarks with sarcastic intent while she stared directly into his eyes. "You don't fool me Herbert; you put much more credence in this than you are letting on."

As the three observers all watched with rapt attention while the two sparred, Constable Manly replied, "You, Ms. Viñas show a lack of respect for the police."

"I show respect when it is due, Constable Manly."

He sighed, got up, stood and stared down at Lynton, "I am warning you all, and especially you Ms. Viñas, to stop your amateurish detecting, and stay the hell out of police business."

"Constable, I originally stayed here at your request. Remember that you told me to stick around, as apparently I am considered a suspect."

"That was the chief's idea at the time, not mine. If it was up to me, I would send you packing. Frankly, I find you an annoyance and your manner extremely disrespectful."

"You know, my husband taught me that respect does not automatically come with wealth, prestige or position. Just because you are a policeman does not bestow respect. Respect is earned, not conferred. Now, we can banter over our mutual dislike for one another all morning, or you can allow me to eat my breakfast, so I can get started with my day, and that tail you have had on me for the last two days can do his job of reporting on my activities. After all, he is just leaning against the wall of the building across the street, collecting taxpayer funds for lounging around. I'll try to make his day interesting, and hopefully make sure he earns his money."

Manly sucked in some air, clinched his teeth and walked out without another word, as Adam looked at his mother and said, "We appear to have a lioness lose in Stellenbosch."

Lynton picked up the menu, looked at it for a split second, put it down and said, "I lost my appetite. You three ready to go with this lion into a den where I may have to roar?"

Perturbed, she continued. "Is your car gassed and ready for the journey to the Krupp estate?"

"Yes," replied Adam.

"I have to shake my police shadow. You three wait for me here."

"How," asked Adam, "are you going to get away from him?"

Lynton smiled and said, "I have my ways." Then she looked down at the table, picked up the thick metal knife and asked Adam to get her a pair of pliers. He excused himself, went into the maintenance closet in the hallway outside the restaurant and came back with the pliers. She had a look of determination, as she got up and said while walking away "Be right back."

The three sat in awe of this remarkable woman who put the knife and pliers in her purse. She pulled her already short skirt up higher on her waist, making it a good ten centremetres above the knee, pulled out her blouse and knotted it around her upper waist, exposing a nice bit of belly flesh, and unbuttoned the first three buttons, displaying some cleavage while Susan was texting on her phone. She walked out the front door, looked across the street, smiled at the detective, waved and gave him a wink. She, as her husband often said, did not walk, but wiggled. She remembered an alley way off Rommel Street and headed in that direction with the detective maybe no more than one hundred feet behind, as he no longer felt the need to hide himself from her.

The detective was tall, barrel-chested, slightly stooping, with high broad shoulders and dressed in a black suit. His face was pale white and wrinkled with dark, deep furrows; his greying hair was sparse and what was left of it was closely cropped. He wore wire-rimmed glasses, and walked with an odd shuffling gait, and, no doubt, his heart was pumping rapidly, not from the chase, but from the view he was enjoying of a seductive woman.

Lynton, who wiggled naturally whenever she walked, this time accentuated the sway, because she knew men were such ninnies, and if she could get this man to concentrate on her womanliness, then he would be easy prey for what she had in mind.

She never looked back, but she sensed he was staring at her with lust, despite the fact that he was still doing his job by following her. She nonchalantly strolled into an alley off Rommel and walked around one hundred feet, where she had, on a previous walk, seen a dumpster. Her follower stopped at the alley entrance and stood there. Even though he had made no attempt to be nondescript while following her, for some reason, maybe because of his leering nature, he hid against a building on his right, peering around the corner.

She placed the purse down in the front and to the right of the dumpster. She lifted the lid on the dumpster and with difficulty, because of her shortness, flipped it all the way back until the top hit the wall behind with a thud. It was open just enough for what she wanted.

She had to be careful, because she had learned long ago that cops and the guns they carried were a lethal combination. She knew what she had to do, but before she did anything, she had to make sure his gun was ineffective.

Curious, the cop could not take his eyes off her and her actions. He thought: "was the woman crazy?" She was, crazy - crazy like a fox.

Lynton stood and waited. She needed to know whether he was right handed or not. Chances were; he was right handed. So, his gun would be on his right hip. She would take a gamble. She smiled broadly and winked at him.

Despite her considerable appealing attributes as a woman, Lynton never took herself too seriously. However, like most women, she knew that manipulating men was relatively easy, as an alluring smile or a come-hither look could disarm them and make them easy to control. The cop was intrigued, and since his cover was already blown, he cautiously strolled down the alley toward the dumpster.

As alluded to in many other Lynton books, she is famed for having what are called high heels from hell, and her strong legs, honed from years as a professional dancer, represent a formable weapon. She was about to lock and load!

The cop made the mistake of getting within about three feet of her, but exercising caution; he pulled back his coat and exposed his gun, putting his right hand on it just to let her know he was prepared for any eventuality. Lynton smiled and went into action.

As he observed her left leg rising, he pulled out his gun. She furiously kicked it out of his hand with one smooth motion. It skidded across the pavement as he momentarily stood in shock that such a little woman could so effectively disarm him. Before he had time to react, Lynton, using her leverage for strength, bent down, grabbed his left leg, lifted him up and tossed him into the open dumpster. She pulled the lid down, reached into her purse and brought out the knife. She slid it into the dumpster latch where a padlock was supposed to go. She took the pliers, and while enduring the curses of the trapped cop, bent the knife with the pliers to secure the latch and make sure he could not jiggle it loose. She said, "If your cell doesn't work, I'll call the police station and tell them where you are. Enjoy your day."

Readjusting her clothes to a less alluring nature, she picked up the gun, unloaded it, walked over to the dumpster, slightly raised the lid and squeezed the gun in. The cop was shouting profanities as she walked away.

Her three compatriots were anxiously waiting. She told Adam to get two large, very sharp butcher knifes for use to remove the two hearts from what would be sleeping vampires during their daytime assault. He came back with them in hand, much to the shock of the customer's in the restaurant.

Lynton said, "Let's get this done, but first I need to use the desk phone, because I don't want to let the police get a bead on my cell and find out where we are. The policeman who was following me might need assistance from headquarters. She called the police and informed them where she had put the policeman. She hung up, smiled at the three and said, "Let's rock and roll gang."

Susan was extremely quiet, and Lynton sitting up front by Adam, who was driving looked back over her left shoulder at her and said, "This may be too difficult for you Susan. Your step mother may be a dead creature of the night, but she is still the woman who reared you, and we can all understand the trepidation you might feel, despite the fact that you are actually doing her a favour by relieving her of the burdens imposed upon her in the constant quest to maintain her immortality. You can wait for us in the car if you like."

Tears were forming in Susan's eyes as she said, "This is not an act of hatred. It is an act of love. This is not killing anyone, as all of them are already dead. We are actually giving them peace. I shall go with you, but I cannot perform the ritual of relief from this horrible life on the one I have called mother." She did not seem sincere, but Lynton, let it go, as it was too late to question her intentions.

LYNTON AND THE STELLENBOSCH TERROR

Of course, Lynton was withholding some secrets from all three. Revealing them before she was 100% sure would only cause anxiousness and misunderstanding. She sensed that there was still more things that were not overtly obvious to her; although, she did have her suspicions on exactly what awaited them. This was not going to be an easy task. She had been laughingly referred to as a lioness by Adam, but the truth was that they were all sheep, including her, about to enter a real lions' den of evil

As the hills where the estate towered high over the valley drew nearer, even in the daylight, there was a feeling of dread as the area was covered with dense forest looming up so darkly and precipitously that one wished they would keep their distance, but there was no road by which to escape them. Across that damnable bridge was a small village huddled between the river and the vertical slope of one tall mountain, and Lynton looked up at the cluster of crows that were circling continuously above. It was not reassuring to see, on a closer glance, that most of the other houses a great distance from the estate were deserted and falling to ruin, and that the broken-steeple church seemed to not be a bulwark against evil, but was seemingly defeated by it. Once across the bridge, it was hard to prevent the impression of a faint, malign odour, as if the massed mould and decay was a testament of the distress suffered by those in the shadow of the Krupp estate.

Outsiders visited the area as seldom as possible, and each time of the year was a season of horror here. Yet, the scenery, judged by any ordinary person, was probably more than commonly normal. Almost a century ago, Myron Krupp had brought evil here along with that young girl who had wandered in the cave near Ypres.

Lynton had, unbeknownst to the three gone one day back to Cape Town and there, in the rare books section of the National Library, read extensively in the archives of half-hidden murders, sacrificial deeds and acts of almost unnameable violence and perversity near Stellenbosch right there on the Krupp estate. No one, even those who had the facts concerning the Stellenbosch horrors, could say just what the problem was. Discourses on the evil at the estate were few, and the connection to a vast number of murders in the town over the years was hinted but never proved. An obscure professor from the University of Cape Town had studied the sinister goings-on, but soon after writing his colleagues with details on his research, he disappeared while at the hotel, and, of course, Lynton knew what had happened to him.

Strange occurrences in the hills about the Krupp estate were ordinary, as was the ghostly appearances at the inn, but no one but Lynton had connected the two. She had also read in the professor's notes of strange night time appearances of two winged creatures and foul odours about the hills near the mansion. Then too, the locals, for years had been mortally afraid of the numerous strange sounds made by the two soaring bats heading toward the estate that often carried what looked like humans in their grasps.

LYNTON AND THE STELLENBOSCH TERROR

As Lynton and her three companions drove slowly across that bridge where the original apparition had appeared, the sun was blotted out by thick black clouds as rain seemed imminent. Lynton motioned for Adam to turn the car to the right after crossing the bridge and park it in a clump of trees at the base of the hill upon which the mansion sat. As they sat in the car, Lynton turned around and said to Susan, "You have been there, and we depend on you to be our guide. You must take us to the room where the coffins lay, but we will have to first disarm and subdue the two males who are obviously more than chauffeurs. They are the guardians of the coffins, the two who protect the premises. We are not here to kill them, but we must make sure they are properly restrained." She then turned to Adam and said, "You got the ropes I requested?"

"I do - in the trunk." he replied.

"Our first mission then is to make sure they are restrained," she said and then looked directly at Susan and continued. "You must distract them."

"My, how do I do that?"

"They know you, so you will walk up to them and tell them that you must see your mother when night falls, and she rises from her death slumber to seek nourishment."

Lynton reached into her purse and came out with a small brown bottle and handed it to her and said, "Throw this in their faces? It is sulphuric ether anaesthesia and will render them unconscious almost immediately. I got it from a chemist in Cape Town when I went to the library one day, as I anticipated it might be needed if we invaded the lair of the vampires. Almost immediately, they will collapse unconscious. They will not have time to assault you. Then Adam and I will tie them up, and we will proceed into the chamber where the coffins are."

Cecile asked, "Are you sure about the number of creatures?"

"No," replied Lynton. "There will be three as Linda is now one of them. However, I suspect there may be a fourth."

"Who is the fourth?" asked Adam.

"I am not 100% sure, but I think it may be someone who died many years ago, but please wait and we shall see if my hunch is right."

They got out of the car and crossed the old dirt road in a very deliberate manner, looking around to make sure no one was observing them, and began their slow and determined ascent up the winding road that led to the estate. To their right and left were masses of trees, long forgotten by time. The seasons had been harsh to them, stripping away the bark from many. When the day passes noon in this area of Stellenbosch the hill and the tops of the trees glisten with a twinkling light from the rays of the sun. The light penetrated through the boughs in shadowy beams and the carcasses of long dead trees felled by the wind teemed with insects working feverishly. There was an intense silence. It was so quiet one could almost hear the beating of one's own heart. There were no movements of animals anywhere about, not even birds in the trees.

LYNTON AND THE STELLENBOSCH TERROR

The forest that was once alive was now as dead as those abominations at the top of the hill in that estate. Although it was mildly warm, all four of the intrepid adventurers felt chilled. The earth beneath the canopy of trees that once seemed alive was parched with death now. The forest was a Wagner symphony, playing funeral dirges for those who had offered the blood of life to the undead dead. This was a forest hugging the evil of that mansion on the hill. It did not care for time. Seconds, minutes, hours and centuries were inconsequential. The smallest measure of time here was the dark cycle of evil.

The fallen leaves and rotting debris sounded like dried cereal being crunched underfoot, pushing their papery remains deep into the soil. The dark shadows flitted about in a dance of the macabre as a strange unnatural mist began to swirl from the forest floor gradually working its way upward until it became so moist, so encompassing that the four looked at one another with a frightful anticipation of what awaited at the top of the hill.

Finally at the top, even the sun could not cast a ray of brightness on the darkness that engulfed that house where evil dwelled. The Hawthornian aspect of the venerable mansion was overpowering. It attacked the psyche with disarmingly chilling effect. It bore not any outwardly expression of light. All about it was a darkness that told of a long lapse of mortal life, and accompanying vicissitudes that have passed within were testament to its evil nature. It was a house that exuded wickedness in the now chilling breeze that hugged the four intruders with moist approbation of the coming battle between good and evil.

Certain houses, like certain people, somehow manage to proclaim a commitment to evil in an unalterable display that malevolence awaits within its interior. The exterior is but a precursor to the evil inside. The malignant gloominess of the place communicated an atmosphere of secret rites and wicked thoughts that danced in an orgy of blood letting within the darkness of its interior.

LYNTON AND THE STELLENBOSCH TERROR

As they started their approach to the front door, suddenly there it was. That same entity that had warned Harold so long ago of impending doom was now manifesting itself before the door into the Krupp mansion. Lynton recognized it immediately and was unafraid, but the other three stood in confusion, for they did not see it.

"What is it?" asked Adam.

"You don't see it?

They all shook their heads no, and then Lynton offered an explanation.

"It is the same as when I saw the professor in the hallway twice when I was talking with you, Adam. I am the only one psychically attuned to its manifestation. Just wait and it will make itself clear. This is a warning not to enter here."

The dark shadowy, cloaked figure floated to the left and moved slowly toward the side of the house. Lynton signalled for the others to follow as she tepidly moved to the side of the house and to a window where the entity paused and then floated upward.

Adam whispered to her, "But it is daylight? How does it come out now?"

Lynton replied, "This entity has the power to manifest itself day or night. Anyway, look around you Adam; look at the darkness of this place. Day or night makes no difference here, how bright the sun shines has no effect on this gloomy testament to evil. This place is in permanent darkness of the soul."

Looking in the window, the two men from that night on the bridge sat at a table playing cards. Lynton whispered. "OK, so we know where they are. Go Susan and dispatch these men with the concoction you have. Adam, get the ropes ready, for we will only have a short time before they will awaken. Go now Susan and good luck."

The dark shadowy cloaked figure floated upward and dissipated. It was not the real Stellenbosch terror, the real terror awaited them within the home where evil had come to dwell.

Chapter 13

Mighty Bulwarks Against Wickedness

Hunter of vampires prowls with sensation.
As the craving of thirst awakens vampire's lure.
Enchanted by the taste of flesh, a night's potion,
His shadow rises upon needs impure.
Enticing one's prey, he offers sinful blessing
To consume blood's feast, the sweetness of nectar,
Another creature now part of the hunter's ring;
Both enshrined by moonlight's conniving star.

Consumed by earthy hunger, fangs devour

LYNTON AND THE STELLENBOSCH TERROR

As seasons feed on eternity's quest,
Not knowing the woman of morning hour
Or sunrise's flavour, gently possessed.
This dead undead craves the luscious bite.
Transcending centuries gothic and old,
He rises in insatiable rabid flight
To search out victims so brazen and bold.

A vampire roams Stellenbosch streets,
Disobeying sanctity's golden condition,
Feasting on whomever it meets
In evil's dancing, dark rendition.
Hell more than heaven is seen,
But Lynton never takes pause.
She walks into the lair of a fiend
With devotion to the cause.

Susan was easily admitted, almost too easily. She was brilliant in rendering the two guards defenceless with the concoction supplied by Lynton. Again, almost too easily. All she did was smile and then splashed them with it, and they coughed twice and collapsed in a heap on the floor. Susan let her three compatriots in and Adam and Lynton quickly tied the two men up, who began to shout obscenities as they regained consciousness. Cecile got two dishcloths and gagged the men. The four began to make their way down into the crypt where the evil ones lay.

It was now nearing 4:00 PM, and Lynton had checked when sundown was. They only had until 5:30 to accomplish their task, and she was not sure how many vampires would be in their slumber. They would have to hurry.

Creeping down the stairs into the dank, dark chamber beneath, to their left lay a grotesque thing half-bent on its side in a foetid pool of greenish-yellow slime. It was quite dead. They gasped in the horror of what they saw there, as has been described earlier. Bits and fragments of apparel were scattered about the room. Near the centre of the room there was an elaborately carved sarcophagus on the right and on the left was a less ornate one. It would be trite and not wholly accurate to say that no human pen could describe the inherent evil and despicable nature of this unsavoury place. There was also a third coffin made of wood that sat between the other two, obviously with an occupant, as part of a white gown hung out of the closed lid, and beside it was a fourth coffin, lid open, obviously awaiting the arrival of another of the undead dead.

Lynton turned to Adam, "Unpack the knives."

Susan stood with a look of determination. She looked over at the portrait that had a large red cloth draped over it. She said to Lynton, "You have a surprise coming."

From behind a black curtain to the left, emerged Constable Manly, gun in hand. He smiled as Susan walked over to him. "Tell them Susan, who the man in the dark cloak and hood was. The one you told them that you could not see."

Smiling and looking at the three, she said, placing her left arm around the Constable, "It was the constable here. You see, his real name is Myron Krupp. It is he who graciously brought my family, which lies in these two coffins here from

Belgium, and it is his bride, Linda, in the wooden coffin."

The constable said to Susan, "Quick, go release our comrades upstairs, because we now have these three right where we want them."

As Susan started up the stairs, Lynton said, "I knew you did not use my concoction on them, because it was nothing but mineral water. You see, this is no surprise to me."

Standing at the top of the stairs, Susan said, "Not true, they were rendered unconscious by the elixir."

Lynton, very assuredly said, "Check what little is left. It is nothing but mineral water. You see, I knew what you were up to, knew you wanted us three dead, because we were all that stood in your way. Well, us and that entity, the ghost of the professor that has tried to thwart your plans every since he tried to warn Harold that night on the road, and in the inn before that. You see, I knew those photos were not a look-a-like, but they were you long ago, when you were alive."

Susan stood dumbfounded, as Lynton continued. "When Adam said he remembered you coming to him in a dream-like state in his childhood that was no dream. It was you. You were there with him, or just happened upon him while with his grandmother." Then she looked over at Adam, "And when you two had a romantic interlude, you noticed she was cold to your touch. Of course she was, because she is dead, but like all Strigoi, which Constable Manly can attest to because he is one, they can walk about in daylight as well as night. The two in the coffins here, Countess Louder and Osiris and now Linda are Strigoi, but still rest at times during the day, so they have the energy to hunt victims at night."

Constable Manly said to Susan, "Quick, get Bob and Frank, and have them come down here. This woman's games are inconsequential, because regardless of what she thinks she knows; these three are all going to be used to satisfy the thirst of our compatriots when they awaken and desire the elixir of life."

LYNTON AND THE STELLENBOSCH TERROR

Susan said to Constable Manly, "She is smart. She has some trick up here sleeve."

"She is not as smart as she thinks she is, because there is another one of us she doesn't know about," offered Constable Manly.

"Oh, I know. I know whose picture is behind that red curtain that is draped over the worst face of evil to ever confront mankind, and I know it is a portrait of who was the world's most abominable human being in all of history, and he is the real reason you are all here, to serve his needs, because he was made into a Strigoi so that one day his evil could rock the foundations of the world."

"Go," barked Manly to Susan. "We need them."

When Susan returned with the two men, she shouted, "Yes, it was only mineral water. They faked it, assuming I had made the substitute."

Lynton let that slow mischievous smile gradually spread across her thick, succulent, ruby red lips, while friend and foe there took deep breaths and stood in awe gazing upon her, wondering what she was up to. She looked as if the light around her was ghost-like, condensed as if she were a lithe gazelle slanting with precision ready to leap across the plain. She was a sleek racing yacht sailing upon the deep blue waters of righteousness, and she exuded peace and serenity with an air of confidence. She was the bright North Star that was the beacon of navigation leading to retribution. She was the sunlight that came up on the morning horizon, the soft cool breeze that floated gently across the pounding waves and made them ripple with the wonder of what awaited. The foam of her sweet, soft voice flew like flaky snow before the wintry tempest of a coming storm. The brightness she shone set course towards tranquility in a calm sea that radiated with her golden haze. This was a woman ready to take on the coming storm with assuredness and confidence.

To Lynton's right were the bodyguards, Frank and Bob. Susan had rejoined Constable Manly over near the coffins. The problem before the vampire slayers was much more than being outnumbered. It was how to deal with three guns now trained on them, as they all waited for the coffins to slowly open and the vampires to emerge for their nourishment.

Lynton looked directly at Susan and said, "The surprise you mentioned is he who is in the portrait behind that curtain. Where is he?"

Susan, amazed at Lynton's perceptiveness, said, "How long have you known?"

"Oh, I knew long ago. The tales of the bats sweeping down upon that battlefield made me realize what was really here, made me realize the true depth of the evil that festers and grows in this place, an evil that has been waiting for a very long time now to rise up from the ashes of history and engulf the world in its malignancy that was started but not finished."

Cecile and Adam were wondering what they were talking about. Lynton looked at them and said, "There is a Strigoi here that is much worse than the vampires lying in the coffins, much worse than the two we are facing now."

With deep emotion, Manly said, "Yes, it is he whom we all serve, because it is he who will unleash fire and fury as the world has never seen, even worse than that buffoon of a U.S. President vowed to unleash on the world. Our master will be exalted again above all others as the world trembles before him and his army of Strigoi who will sweep across the world to bring all to their knees before this living god, this monarch of mayhem."

Death can be so beautiful - to lie in the soft brown earth with the grasses waving above one's head, and listen to silence, to have no yesterday and no tomorrow, to forget time, to forget life, to be at peace. For some people, death is not something to fear, but something to look forward to. Susan and Manly, along with the three creatures in the coffins, had never known the peace of death. It had been snatched from them. Lynton looked directly at Manly as she saw a dark hooded figure fluttering above the ceiling. She smiled. The friendly entity was there to help.

LYNTON AND THE STELLENBOSCH TERROR

The figure suddenly engulfed the two in a swirling whirlwind, and Manly dropped his gun. At the exact same time, Lynton pivoted on her right foot, raising her left leg waist high and with her famous high heels from hell rammed her left heel into Bob's groin, causing him to drop the gun while falling to the floor in excruciating pain. In the same motion, she extended her right hand in a flicking movement to deflect the gun in Frank's left hand just as it fired. The bullet tore into Bob's flesh as he lay on the floor. He looked upward, closed his eyes and died.

Frank dived for the gun that had dropped to the floor, wrestling over it with Adam. It went off again as they struggled, the bullet entering under Frank's chin and exiting the top of his head. Adam, the gun in his hand turned it toward Manly who was still wrapped in the dark shadow and swirling around in the whirlwind along with Susan. He fired one shot at him.

Lynton, as she reached into Adam's bag, shouted, "You can't shoot a vampire."

She quickly removed the one thing that Adam had questioned her about as they met privately, away from the prying eyes of Susan, to prepare for battle in the vampires' lair. A nail gun seemed an unusual item to bring to a vampire fight, and when she had dipped each nail in a vat of molten silver, she explained that in order to render a Strigoi immobile, a nail tipped in solid silver driven into its forehead was a necessity.

As Cecile stood in awe of Adam and Lynton's tenaciousness in battle, Lynton moved toward the whirlwind that was now ceasing. Manly moved forward swiftly to retrieve the gun, but she was swifter, as she took aim with the nail gun and the silver tipped nail pierced his forehead, making him drop to the floor just as Susan realized her own fate was now at hand. She knew it was over. She did not tarry in fear, but stood erect looking directly into Lynton's eyes, as Lynton raised the nail gun and the silver tipped nail pounded into her forehead. Lynton stood triumphant. She sighed and said, "Now the dirty work."

LYNTON AND THE STELLENBOSCH TERROR

All of us encompass heaven and hell in a world where it is difficult to tell the two apart. But there are many heavens and, unfortunately, many more hells. The artist snatches fire from both, which is what this writer is attempting to do here. Surely the assassin feels no more intensely the lust of murder than the writer who depicts it in glowing words. The things I write here are as real to me as the stars that twinkle in the night. I shall not overly parley the despicably disgusting blood bath that was wrought upon the five corpses of the creatures of the night by these grand heroes as each of their two hearts were meticulously dissected, burned and buried. Their devotion to saving Stellenbosch from the terror wrought by these evil ones transcends the limits of this grossly inadequate writer to effectively describe them.

The throngs in town would never know how many lives might have been saved by the actions of these three people who braved annihilation at the hands of the undead dead. These were three unsung heroes, and also there was a fourth!

As their ghastly chore of sealing the fate of the creatures was completed, the fourth member of this grand group once again floated above them. The three stood in gratefulness below the floating professor's ghost, which was a symbol of too often misjudging the intent of others, mistaking good for evil. Lynton, with the entity floating overhead, said, "Being against evil doesn't make you good. Tonight I was against it and then I was evil myself in what I had to do. I could feel it coming just like a tide. I just wanted to destroy them. But when you start taking pleasure in it you are awfully close to the thing you're fighting. I see their evil, but I take no pleasure in what had to be done to eradicate it. All the professor ever wanted was to offer a warning to those who were going to be the prey of these evil creatures of the night. It had been his work in both life and death. He is at peace now."

They all looked upward at the dark shadowy figure as it slowly dissipated. The three felt relief that his ghost was now free to move on, because the terror had been stayed, in no small part, due to his over 100 years of effort that had so often been terribly misconstrued.

These three felt a sense of peacefulness and tranquility as the entity was finally able to complete its mission. Lynton said, "We must clean up anything that might point to the fact we were here. Explaining to the authorities what we did might put us in a mental institution."

As they cleaned up, Lynton observed with glee Adam and Cecile scurrying about. She had found two devoted, loyal, dedicated companions in the fight for justice in a world where it was far too often overwhelmed by evil.

When contemplation and reflection are stored in the heart of the worthy, the whole globe is but one great dewdrop of hope that flies through the great cosmos singing and shining with the glory of the brave few who refuse to bow before evil. In a world where evil triumphs every day by keeping billions in poverty so a few can enjoy lives of splendorous luxury, and where the evil of greed is promoted as good to excuse the selfish actions of those at the top of the economic ladder, these three stood as mighty bulwarks against wickedness.

Epilogue
One Strigoi Escaped

She has the bravest eyes ever seen.
Lions bow before her, shivering in fear.
She is the one in whom the downtrodden believe;
Beautiful, defiant and forever gloriously free.
This is a woman who makes vampires flee.
She never cowers before evil in any form.
Defeating the Stellenbosch terror was her aim,
And now she has lit good's bright flame!

Lynton's life is a life of danger. She pursues honour on the mountain of hope and finds it far too rarely in a world based upon privilege for the few at the expense of the many. She is in a constant battle against evil that is the raging storm encircling all humanity in the grasp of those who will never willingly reach out with compassion to the suffering throngs. Still, despite overwhelming odds against her pursuit of justice, she displays a distinguished chivalry that elevates her to an exalted status among those who look to her for help. She is adored as a woman who never shirks from fighting evil, whether it is the wickedness of an economic system based on greed, a political dynasty of damnable cretins in service to the privileged class, money-grubbing charlatans of religious subterfuge or any of the other multitudes of miscreants who prey upon the weak and vulnerable. Or, of course, the vampires and other despicable creatures that feast upon the unsuspecting in their lust to feed their evil. Once again, as she stands triumphant, she is the envy of those who long for one small semblance of her courage to course through their veins.

LYNTON AND THE STELLENBOSCH TERROR

It is she who knows it is not light that is always needed, but a raging fire; the rumbling shower of lightning that with accompanying roaring thunder will make the evil ones know that retribution is on its way. Sometimes justice requires the storm, the whirlwind and the earthquake.

As they prepared to leave the lair of evil, just as they started to ascend the steps, Adam said as he pointed over to that portrait that was covered by a red drape, "But what of the other vampire? What of the person in that portrait?"

"Unfortunately," said a somewhat despondent Lynton, "I know he has escaped, because he feared the coming calamity. His is an evil that was born in the trenches of World War I when two Strigoi swept down on a battlefield in Belgium and made him into one of their own. His is an evil that was proclaimed dead for all time when it was assumed he committed suicide. He survived a burning of his body, because you cannot kill a Strigoi by flames. How he got here I do not know, but his evil seems to live on and on."

Adam said, "He is like the others then, he can only be killed by removing his hearts and cutting them in two as we have done, but who is he? I must know."

Adam strolled over to the portrait and pulled off the curtain. Evil stared him in the face, an evil that was still loose on the earth. Still free somewhere to wreck havoc on the unsuspecting. Oh my, there was one Strigoi that had escaped them. It was Adolph Hitler!

The End Or Is It?

LYNTON AND THE STELLENBOSCH TERROR

Don't miss my
other adventures
from
J. Wayne Frye
and
Fireside Books.

The Lynton Series

#1 Lynton Curls Her Hair
#2 Lynton Buys a Cell-Phone and Hears the Voice of Doom
#3 Lynton and the Vampire at Tagaytay Manor
#4 Lynton Walks on Water
#5 Lynton and the Ghosts in the Mansion on Balete Drive
#6 Lynton Viñas and Beowulf Perez in the Taal Inferno
#7 Pursuit (Adults Only)
#8 Chablis and Lynton in the Room of Doom (Adults Only)
#9Lynton Viñas: Demon Fighter in Black and White
#10 Lynton Viñas: Shadow in the Darkness
#11 Lynton's South African Adventure
 # 12 Lynton, the Karoo Vampire and the Jewels of Omar Bin Abi

Other Adventures of Interest for Those
Who Enjoyed This Book

Hockey Mania and the Mystery of Nancy Running Elk
How Hockey Saved a Jew From the Holocaust
White Meteors and the Ghost of Sue Ann McGee
Sammy Sasquatch and the Sts'ailes Star

J. WAYNE FRYE

www.ingramcontent.com/pod-product-compliance
Lightning Source LLC
Chambersburg PA
CBHW070553130626
46556CB00001B/144